Ten Plus One

Ed McBain was born in Manhattan, but fled to the Bronx
at the age of twelve. He went through elementary and high
school in the New York City school system, and the Navy
claimed him in 1944. When he returned two years later he
attended Hunter College. After a variety of jobs, he worked
for a literary agent, where he learnt about plotting stories.
When his agent-boss started selling them regularly to
magazines, and sold a mystery novel and a juvenile
science-fiction title as well, they both decided that it would
be more profitable for him to stay at home and write full
time.

Under his own name, Evan Hunter, he is the author of
a number of novels, including *The Blackboard Jungle*,
Come Winter and *Every Little Crook and Nanny*. As Ed
McBain he has written the highly popular '87th Precinct'
series of crime novels, including *Shotgun*, *Jigsaw*, *Fuzz*,
Doll, *Bread* and *Like Love*, all of which are available
in Pan.

D0996188

Also by Ed McBain in Pan Books

Bread
Like Love
Doll
Axe
Eighty Million Eyes
He Who Hesitates
Shotgun
Jigsaw
Fuzz
Hail, Hail, the Gang's All Here!
Sadie When She Died
Let's Hear It for the Deaf Man
Hail to the Chief
So Long as You Both Shall Live
Long Time No See
Calypso
The Empty Hours
Ghosts
Heat
Lady, Lady, I Did It
The McBain Brief

Ed McBain

Ten plus one

An 87th Precinct Mystery
Pan Books London and Sydney

First published in Great Britain 1964 by Hamish Hamilton Ltd
This edition published 1975 by
Pan Books Ltd, Cavaye Place, London SW10 9PG
9
© Ed McBain 1963
ISBN 0 330 24116 8
Printed in England by Clays Ltd, St Ives plc

This is for Herbert Alexander

Chapter One

Nobody thinks about death on a nice spring day.

Autumn is the time for dying, not spring. Autumn encourages macabre thoughts, invites the ghoulish imagination, tempts the death-wish with sere and withered evidence of decay. Autumn is poetic as hell, brief, succinct, stinking of mould and ashes. People die a lot in autumn. Everything dies a lot in autumn.

Nothing is allowed to die in the spring. There's a law that says so – Penal Law 5,006, DEATH IN THE SPRING: 'Whosoever shall expire, or cause to expire, or conspire to expire, or harbour thoughts of expiring during the vernal equinox shall be guilty of a felony punishable by ...' It goes on like that. It absolutely forbids death between March 21 and June 21, but there are lawbreakers everywhere, so what can you do?

The man who stepped out of the office building on Culver Avenue was about to become a lawbreaker. Normally, he was a good citizen, a hard-working man, a faithful husband, a devoted father, all that jazz. He had no intention of breaking the law. He didn't know that death was forbidden by legislature, but even if he *had* known, it wouldn't have concerned him, because death and dying were the furthest things from his mind on that bright spring day.

He was, in fact, thinking of life. He was thinking that next week was his birthday, that he would be forty-five years old, that he didn't feel a day over thirty-five. He was thinking that the grey at his temples added a corny but distinguished touch to his noble head, that his shoulders were still broad, that his twice-weekly tennis sessions had eliminated an alarming little potbelly, and that he would lay his wife the moment he saw her, even if they'd never be allowed to eat at Schrafft's again.

He was thinking all these things when the bullet sang across the open, fresh, spring air, spiralling wickedly, unglintingly,

7

unerringly accurate as it traversed the area from the roof of the building across the street, high above the tops of the beetle cars and the heads of the ant people enjoying spring, fast, true, deadly, to the sidewalk opposite, to hit him between the eyes.

Only one thought flashed into his mind the second the bullet struck, and then all thought ceased. He felt a single sharp shattering blow between his eyes and he thought for a split instant that he had walked into the glass doors that separated the building from the street outside. The bullet splintered through bone, found the soft cushion of his brain, and then blew a hole the size of a baseball through the back of his head as it passed on through. Thought stopped, feeling stopped, there was suddenly nothing. The impact sent him reeling back three feet to collide with a young girl in a yellow cotton frock. He fell backwards as the girl reflexively sidestepped, his body seemed to fold in on itself like a battered accordion, the tennis muscles relaxed, he was dead even before he hit the pavement. The large hole below his forehead leaked a tiny trickle of blood while the enormous exit hole at the base of his skull poured blood onto the sidewalk steadily, wetly, redly, a blinding, screaming red still hot with life, flowing swiftly to where the girl stood in shocked and dumb horror, watching the stream of blood as it rushed across the sidewalk.

She pulled back her foot just in time; in another moment, the blood would have touched the toe of her high-heeled pump.

*

Detective Steve Carella looked down at the body on the sidewalk, and wondered how it could be that ten minutes ago when he left the precinct there were no flies, it was too early in the season for flies, and that now, as he looked down at the dead man whose blood had stopped flowing, the pavement was covered with flies, there was a swarm of flies in the air, and another half-dozen flies were feeding at the open hole between the man's eyes.

'Can't you cover him up?' he snapped at one of the internes, and the interne shrugged and gestured innocently towards the police photographer who was putting another roll of film into his camera in the shade of the ambulance parked at the kerb.

Without looking up, the photographer said, 'Got to take his picture.'

Carella turned away from the body. He was a tall man with a fine-honed muscular appearance, high cheekbones, his brown hair cut sparingly, his brown eyes slanting peculiarly downward to give his face a pained and suffering oriental look as he turned into the sun, squinting, and walked to where the girl in the yellow frock was talking to several newspaper reporters.

'Later, boys,' he said, and the newspapermen, oddly quiescent in the presence of death, faded back into the circle of bystanders beyond the fringe of patrolmen.

'How do you feel?' Carella asked.

'All right. Gee,' she said. 'Gee.'

'Do you feel like answering a few questions?'

'Sure. Gee, I never saw anything like this in my life before. Wait'll I tell my husband.'

'What's your name, ma'am?'

'Mrs Irving Grant.'

'Your first name?'

'Lizanne. With a z.'

'And your address, Mrs Grant?'

'Eleven forty-two Grover.' She paused. 'That's below First.'

'Mmm,' Carella said, jotting the address into his book.

'I mean, in case you thought I lived in a Puerto Rican neighbourhood.'

'No, I didn't think that,' Carella said. He was suddenly very tired. There was a dead man covered with flies on the pavement, and a possible witness to the shooting was worried about whether or not he would think she lived in a Puerto Rican neighbourhood. He wanted to explain that he didn't give a damn whether she lived in a Puerto Rican neighbourhood or a Czechoslovakian neighbourhood, so long as she could tell him, with minimal emotion and maximal accuracy, what she had seen happen to the dead man, who no longer had a nationality. He gave her an over-the-pencil glance that he hoped was withering enough, and then he said, 'Can you tell me what happened?'

'Who is he?' Mrs Grant asked.

'We don't know yet. We haven't looked him over for identification. I'm waiting until the photographer is finished. Can you tell me what happened?'

'I was just walking along when he bumped into me.' She

9

shrugged. 'Then he fell down, and I looked at him, and he was bleeding. Gee, I'm telling you, I never . . .'

'What do you mean he bumped into you?'

'Well, he *backed* into me, really.'

'He'd been shot already, is that it? And he fell backwards against you?'

'I don't know if he'd been shot. I guess he had.'

'Well, did he stumble backwards, or fall, or what?'

'I don't know. I wasn't paying any attention. I was walking along, that's all, when he bumped into me.'

'All right, Mrs Grant, what happened then?'

'Then he just fell over backwards. I moved away from him, and I looked down at him, and that was when I saw he was bleeding, and I knew he was hurt.'

'What'd you do?'

'I don't know what I did. I just kept looking at him, I think.' She shook her head. 'Wait'll I tell my husband about this.'

'Did you hear the shot, Mrs Grant?'

'No.'

'You're certain you didn't hear anything?'

'I was walking along thinking my own thoughts,' Mrs Grant said. 'I didn't expect a thing like this to happen. I mean, maybe there was a shot, maybe there were six shots, I'm only saying I didn't hear anything. He bumped into me all of a sudden, and then he fell down, and there was blood all over his face. Urghh.' Mrs Grant grimaced at the memory.

'I don't suppose you saw anyone with a gun?'

'A gun? No. A what? A gun? No, no.'

'I know you were busy thinking your own thoughts before the man got shot, but *afterwards*, Mrs Grant? Did you see anyone in one of the windows across the way, or perhaps on the roof of one of the buildings? Did you notice anything unusual?'

'I didn't look around,' Mrs Grant said. 'I just kept staring at his face.'

'Did the man say anything to you before he fell to the sidewalk?'

'Not a word.'

'*After* he fell?'

'Nothing.'

'Thank you, Mrs Grant,' Carella said. He smiled briefly but pleasantly and then closed his notebook.

'Is that all?'

'Yes, thank you.'

'But ...' Mrs Grant seemed disappointed. She gave a slight shrug.

'Yes, Mrs Grant?'

'Well ... won't I have to come to the trial or anything?'

'I don't think so, Mrs Grant. Thank you very much.'

'Well ... all right,' Mrs Grant said, but she kept watching him in disappointment as he walked away from her and back to the body. The police photographer was dancing his intricate little jig around the corpse, snapping a picture, ejecting a flash-bulb, inserting another flash-bulb, and then twisting his body and bending his knees to get a shot from another angle. The two internes stood near the ambulance, casually smoking and chatting about an emergency tracheotomy one had performed the day before. Not three feet away from them, talking to a patrolman, stood detectives Monoghan and Monroe, who had been sent over as a matter of form from Homicide North. Carella watched the photographer for a moment, and then walked over to the two Homicide dicks.

'Well, well,' he said, 'to what do we owe the honour?'

Monoghan, wearing a black topcoat and a black derby, looking like a Prohibition cop of the twenties, turned, looked at Carella, and then said to Monroe, 'Why, it's Carella of the eight-seven,' as though discovering him in great surprise.

'Upon my soul, I believe it is,' Monroe said, turning away from the patrolman. He, too, wore a black topcoat. A grey fedora was pushed onto the back of his head. He had a nervous tic near one eye that seemed to jerk magically whenever his partner spoke, as though a secret recording mechanism were at work behind his fleshy features.

'I hope we didn't break in on your dinner or anything,' Carella said.

'What I like about the cops of the Eighty-seventh,' Monoghan said while Monroe ticked, 'is that they are always so concerned about their colleagues in the department.'

'Also, they are very funny,' Monroe observed.

'I am always amazed,' Monoghan said, putting his hands in his coat pockets, with the thumbs sticking out, the way he had seen it done by Sydney Greenstreet in a movie once, 'by their concern and their good humour.'

'I am always amazed by it, too,' Monroe said.

'Who's the stiff?' Monoghan asked.

'Don't know yet,' Carella replied. 'I'm waiting for the photographer to get finished there.'

'He takes a good picture,' Monroe said.

'He does portrait work on the side, I hear,' Monoghan said.

'You know what some of these guys are doing now?' Monroe asked.

'Which guys?' Monoghan said.

'The photographers. The ones they send out on homicides.'

'No. What are they doing?'

'They're using these polaroid cameras to take their pictures.'

'Yeah? What's their hurry?'

'It ain't that they're in any hurry,' Monroe said, 'it's just that when you're working with a stiff, like if the picture don't turn out, you can't call him back for another sitting, you know? By that time, the morgue's got him all cut up. So this way, the photographers can see what they got right off.'

'Boy, what they won't think of next, huh?' Monoghan said, properly awed. 'So what's new, Carella? How's the skipper? How're the boys?'

'Everybody's fine,' Carella said.

'You working on anything interesting?'

'This ought to be an interesting one,' Carella said.

'Yeah, snipers are always interesting,' Monoghan agreed.

'We had a sniper once,' Monroe said, 'when I was just made detective, working out of the three-nine. He used to shoot only old ladies. That was his speciality, little old ladies. He used to pick them off with a forty-five. He was a damn good shot, too. You remember Mickey Dunhill?'

'Yeah, I remember him,' Monoghan said.

'You remember Mickey Dunhill?' Monroe asked Carella.

'No. Who's Mickey Dunhill?'

'Detective/first working out of the three-nine. Little tiny guy, he could knock you flat on your ass, strong as an ox. We dressed him up like a little old lady. That's how we got the guy. He took a shot at Dunhill, and Dunhill pulled up his skirts and chased him up the roof and nearly beat him to death.'

'Yeah, I remember,' Monoghan said.

'We get the guy downtown, you know? The sniper? We put him in a chair, we try to find out how come he's killing little old ladies. We figure maybe he's got an Oedipus thing, you know? But ...'

'A *what*?' Monoghan asked.

'Oedipus,' Monroe said. 'He was this Greek king. He slept with his old lady.'

'That's against the law,' Monoghan said.

'I know. Anyway, we figured maybe this sniper was nuts, you know? So we kept asking him how come little old ladies? Why don't he pick on little old men? Or *anybody*, for that matter? How come he only plugs sweet little old ladies?'

'How come?' Monoghan asked.

Monroe shrugged. 'He wouldn't tell us.'

'What do you mean?'

'He wouldn't tell us.'

'So what's the point of your story?'

'What do you mean, what's the point? Here was a guy, he used to go around shooting little old ladies!' Monroe said indignantly.

'Yeah? So?'

'So? So, what do you mean, what's the point? *That's* the point.'

'What about the other guy?'

'What guy?'

'The Greek guy,' Monoghan said impatiently.

'What Greek guy?'

'The king, the king. Didn't you say there was a Greek king?'

'Oh, for God's sake, he had nothing to do with it,' Monroe said.

'You shoulda looked him up, anyway,' Monoghan insisted. 'You never know.'

'How could we look him up? He was legendary.'

'He was what?' Monoghan asked.

'Legendary. Legendary.'

13

Monoghan nodded knowingly. 'Well, that could make a difference,' he said. 'Still, it always pays to cover all the angles.'

'I think the photographer's through,' Carella said.

'You need us?' Monroe asked.

'I don't think so. I'll send you a copy of the report.'

'You know what you should do?' Monroe said.

'What?'

'Dress up that big redhead you got up there, what's his name?'

'Cotton Hawes?'

'Yeah, him. Dress him up like a little old lady. Maybe your sniper'll take a crack at him.'

'He seems to favour middle-aged men,' Carella said.

Monoghan turned to look at the corpse. 'He can't be more than forty,' he said, slightly miffed. 'Since when is forty middle-aged?'

'Mature, I meant,' Carella said.

'Yeah, that's better,' Monoghan answered. 'Send us *two* copies, we got a new regulation.'

'Come on, have a heart,' Carella said.

'Do I make the regulations?'

'You mean you *don't*?' Carella said, looking surprised.

'There he goes again. See what I mean? You could wet your pants laughing. Send the two copies, Carella. See who gets the last laugh.'

'You think maybe the Greek guy did it?' Carella asked.

'What Greek guy?'

'I don't know, the one Monroe was talking about.'

'I wouldn't put it past him,' Monoghan said. 'A guy who'd sleep with his own mother is capable of anything.'

Smiling, Carella walked to where the photographer was packing his equipment. 'You all finished here?' he asked.

'Be my guest,' the photographer said.

'I'll want some of those pictures.'

'Sure. What precinct is this, anyway?'

'The eight-seven.'

'Right,' the photographer said. 'And your name?'

'Carella. Steve Carella.'

'You'll have them tomorrow.' He glanced at the sedan that pulled to the kerb and then grinned and said, 'Uh-oh.'

'What's the matter?'

'The lab boys. Now you'll have to wait till *they* get through.'

'All I want to do is find out who the hell the guy *is*,' Carella said, and then he turned towards the two technicians who stepped out of the automobile.

Chapter Two

He had found out who the hell the guy was by going through his wallet, and now the hard part lay ahead.

The guy was Anthony Forrest, and his driver's licence gave his address as 301 Morrison Drive, his height as five feet eight inches, and his eyes as blue. He carried six credit cards, all made out to Anthony Forrest: the Diner's Club, American Express, Carte Blanche, the Gulf Oil Corporation, the Mobil Oil Company, and a card for one of the men's department stores in the city. He also carried a business card which repeated his name, Anthony Forrest, and gave the name of his firm, Indian Exports, Inc., and the address, 580 Culver Avenue, which happened to be the address of the building in front of which he'd been shot and killed. The business card also gave him a title, which was Vice-President, and a phone number for the company, Frederick 7–4100. There were assorted other cards and scraps of paper in his wallet, and a five-dollar bill folded into his driver's licence, apparently there as insurance against traffic tickets. There were seventy dollars in cash in the wallet, three twenties, the five and five singles.

Carella found the photographs in the gatefold.

The woman was perhaps thirty-five years old, with bright youthful eyes and light hair. She smiled happily up at him through the celluloid case. There were pictures of three different children, all with the woman's light hair and light eyes, two boys and a girl. The boys were wearing Cub Scout uniforms. One seemed to be slightly older than the other, but neither one was more than ten or eleven. The girl was perhaps fifteen or sixteen. The picture of her had been taken at a beach some place. She was holding a large, striped beach-ball and grinning over its top. Forrest himself stood behind her, grinning like a teenager, holding up two fingers behind her head so that they resembled horns.

Carella sighed and closed the wallet.

There is a quaint police regulation which requires corpses to be identified, and it is usually a blood relative who makes the positive identification, thereby enabling the police to know they are looking for the murderer of John Smith rather than the murderer of John Doe. The pictures in the wallet seemed to indicate that Forrest had a wife and three children, and it now remained for somebody to go to his home, wait for his door to open, face that wife and those children, and tell them that Anthony Forrest, husband, father, loved one, was stone cold dead.

The somebody was Steve Carella.

*

The girl who opened the door at 301 Morrison was the same girl Carella had seen grinning over the top of the beach-ball in the photograph. The picture, though, had obviously been taken some years before, because the girl seemed to be at least nineteen or twenty. Her hair didn't seem as blonde, either, but there was the same lively inquiry in her blue eyes, and she smiled at Carella in polite confusion and said, 'Yes? May I help you?'

'Miss Forrest?' Carella asked.

'Yes?' she said, more confused now, the blonde eyebrows rising ever so slightly on her forehead.

'I'm Detective Carella of the Eighty-seventh Precinct,' Carella said. He paused, obligingly showed his shield and his ID card, and then cleared his throat. The girl waited. 'May I speak to your mother, please?'

'She's not in,' the girl said.

'Do you know where I can reach her?'

'She went to meet my father for dinner,' the girl said. 'Why?'

'Oh,' Carella said, and suddenly the girl got the message. Up to that moment she had been only puzzled by his appearance, but something in the way he said the word 'Oh' triggered alarm in her, and her eyes opened wide, and she took a short, quick step towards him and said, 'What is it?'

'May I come in, please?'

'Yes, certainly,' the girl said, but they did not move farther into the house than the entrance foyer. 'What is it?' she said. 'What happened?'

'Miss . . .' Carella said, and he hesitated, wondering if he should tell her, wondering if she was old enough to hear this, and yet realizing he had to locate her mother, had to inform *someone*.

'Do you know where your mother went? Where she was going to meet him?'

'Yes, Schrafft's. I don't know if they were going to have dinner there, but that's where they were meeting. Look, will you please tell me what this is about?'

Carella looked at her for what seemed like a very long time. Then, very gently, he said, 'Miss, your father is dead.'

The girl backed away from him. She stared at him a moment, and then smiled curiously, and then the smile dropped from her mouth, and she shook her head once, briefly, and said, 'No.'

'I'm sorry, miss.'

'There must be some mistake. He was meeting my mother for . . .'

'I don't think there's any mistake, miss.'

'Well ... well ... how do you *know*? I mean ... for God's sake, what happened?'

'He was shot.'

'My *father*?' she asked incredulously. She shook her head again. 'Shot? Are you joking or something?'

'I'm sorry, miss, I'm not joking. I'd like to contact your mother. May I use your phone?'

'Look ... look ... what you said is ... is impossible, don't you see? My father's name is Anthony Forrest. Now I'm sure you've . . .'

Carella touched her arm gently. 'Miss,' he said, 'the man was carrying identification. We're reasonably certain he was your father.'

'What sort of identification?'

'A wallet.'

'Then someone must have stolen it from him,' the girl said. 'That happens all the time, you know. And the man who got shot was undoubtedly carrying my father's stolen wallet, so naturally you assumed . . .'

'Who is it, Cindy?' a boy's voice yelled from somewhere upstairs.

'It's nothing, Jeff. It's all right,' she answered.

'I'd like to call your mother,' Carella said.

'Why? So you can alarm *her* unnecessarily, too?'

Carella did not answer. He stared at the girl in silence. Tears were gathering behind her eyes, he could see them gathering, but she held on tightly for several moments and then said, 'Go ahead, call. But ... you better be right, you hear me? That man better be my father. Because ... you ... you just better not be making any mistake.' The tears were standing in her eyes now, an opaque film over the clear blue. 'The phone's in here,' she said. As he followed her into the living-room, she added, 'I'm sure he's not my father.' A small laugh caught in her throat. 'What would my father be doing getting ... getting shot?'

Carella picked up the phone book and looked up the number of the Schrafft's restaurant closest to Forrest's business office. He was starting to dial when the girl touched his hand.

'Listen,' she said.

He looked up.

'Listen,' she said, and the tears suddenly began rolling down her face uncontrollably, 'she's not a very strong woman. Please ... when you tell her ... please do it gently? Please? When you tell her my father is dead? Please?'

Carella nodded and began dialling the number.

*

Clara Forrest was thirty-nine years old, a slender woman with a network of tiny wrinkles around her eyes and her mouth. She accompanied Carella into the mortuary silently, her face fixed in that curiously tight, almost angry, expression people assume when they are told death has arrived. While the attendant pulled out the drawer on its oiled rollers, she stood by silently and then looked silently into the face of her husband, and nodded only once. She had accepted the knowledge the moment Carella revealed it on the telephone. This now, this looking into the face of the man she had married when she was nineteen, the man she had loved since she was seventeen, the man to whom she had borne three children, the man she had seen through bad times and good, this now, this looking into the dead and sightless face of a man who was now a corpse on an oiled drawer in a mortuary, this was only routine. The heartache had started the moment Carella spoke the words to her, and the rest was only routine.

'Is that your husband, Mrs Forrest?' Carella asked.

'Yes.'

'And his name is Anthony Forrest?'

'Yes.' Clara shook her head. 'Can we get out of here, please?'

They walked out of the big, echoing room and stood outside in the hospital corridor.

'Will they do an autopsy?' she asked.

'Yes, Mrs Forrest.'

'I wish they wouldn't.'

'I'm sorry.'

'Do you think it was painful for him?'

'He probably died instantly, Mrs Forrest.'

'Thank God for that.'

There was a long silence.

'We have clocks,' Clara said. 'Oh, maybe two dozen of them. I knew this would happen.'

'What do you mean?'

'He always wound the clocks. Some of them are very complicated. The older ones. And some of the tricky foreign ones. He used to wind them every week, on Saturday, all the clocks.' She paused and smiled tiredly. 'I was always so afraid this would happen. You see, he . . . I never learned how to wind them.'

'I don't understand,' Carella said.

'Now . . . now that Tony's gone,' she said dully, 'who'll wind the clocks?'

And then she began weeping.

*

The police department is a vast organization, and a detective is only an organization man. He goes to his office each day, and he conducts his business. And, as with any other business, there are company rules and company procedures, and papers to be typed and dictated, and phone calls to be made, and people to be interviewed and visited, and facts to be researched, and other branches of the organization to contact, and specialists to be consulted. And, as with any other business, it is impossible in police work to devote one's full energies to a single pressing matter. There are always calls about something else, there are always unrelated people to see, there are conflicting vacation schedules and shortages of personnel, and overlapping and backslipping, and plain weariness.

Being a detective is something like being an account executive.

There is only one substantial difference, and once the mental adjustment is made, the difference becomes negligible.

An account executive, despite the cut-throat notoriety of his profession, rarely has to look death in the face, and certainly does not have to look it in the face daily.

A detective sees death in all its various forms at least five times a week, and usually more often. He sees it in the street in its elemental form, the slow disintegration of boys and girls, men and women, exposed to the rotting decay of the slums, dying bit by bit, having the life sucked out of them by the relentless city. He sees it more viciously in the junkies, a death that exists only by its negation of life, the slow suffocation of all will, the gradual extinction of any drive save the drive towards heroin. He sees it in convicted thieves, the burglars, the muggers, the con men, the pimps, a death imposed by law, the gradual death of confinement behind bars. He sees it in the whores who have witnessed the death of honour, and daily multiply the death of love, who bleed away their own lives fifty times a day beneath the relentless stabbings of countless conjugations. He sees it in the homosexuals, who have watched their manhood die, and who live a desperate dying life in the shadow of the law. He sees it in the juvenile street gangs, who live in fear of death and who propagate fear by inflicting death to banish fear.

And he sees it at its worst, as the result of violent emotions bursting into the mind and erupting from the hands. He sees gunshot wounds and stab wounds and hatchet wounds and ice-pick wounds and mutilations and eviscerations. And each time, each time he looks at another human body that has been killed and nullified, he is yanked out of his own body, loses his own humanity to become an observer, a visitor from somewhere far in space studying a curious race of insect people who rip each other apart, who tear each other limb from limb and drink each other's blood; he stands appalled, a civilized human who momentarily renounces his citizenship, unable to believe such cruelty can exist in men who have almost reached the stars. And then he blinks his eyes shut, and he opens them again, and there is only a case lying on the pavement, and he is only an organization man, and there are facts to be dug for and information to be had, before this one can be filed away with all the rest.

*

The ballistics report informed Carella that the bullet dug from the wooden runner of the doors behind Forrest and the discharged shell found on the rooftop of the building across the way were separate parts of a .308-calibre Remington cartridge. The report also stated that the .308 had a full metal case, with a copper-jacketed bullet that had six lands and grooves, a soft point, a right twist, and weighed 191·6 grains. It was suggested that Forrest's murderer must have used a telescopic sight, the distance from the roof to the sidewalk where Forrest was standing being something over a hundred and fifty yards.

Carella studied the report, and then behaved like a man who had not been in this business for a long long time. He ignored the nagging premonition that had begun the moment he looked down at the dead man, in the hope that if he ignored it, it would go away, thereby making the case easier to cope with. He had caught the squeal, and so the case was officially his. The men of the 87th rarely worked with a fixed partner, rather sharing the caseload in a haphazard but effective manner, delegating duty to whoever had time or energy to spare. It was only April, but Meyer Meyer was just returning from his vacation to replace Bert Kling, who was leaving on his. The early vacations were the lieutenant's idea; gang violence and crime in general seemed to enjoy an upswing during the summer months, and he wanted his full squad on duty during July and August. Cotton Hawes and Hal Willis were desperately trying to crack a series of warehouse robberies, Andy Parker was working on a jewellery hold-up, and Arthur Brown was working with the Narcotics Squad in an attempt to flush out a known pusher hiding in the precinct. There were sixteen detectives on the squad, and Carella had worked with them all at one time or another, but he enjoyed working with Meyer Meyer and was happy when the lieutenant assigned him to the case.

Meyer, oddly, fell immediately into the pattern Carella had set. He, too, blatantly ignored something that was staring them both in the face. He seemed inordinately glad to discover that they knew who the victim was, where his family lived, and what kind of bullet had killed him. They had often begun cases without the faintest idea of the victim's name or address, without a single clue to his family or friends.

They told each other they were looking for a specific human being who had slain another specific human being. They knew very well that it was impossible to crack every murder case that came their way, but they also knew that the proper amount of patience and legwork, coupled with the right questions posed to the right people, usually brought about the desired results. A man, they told themselves, doesn't get killed unless someone feels he should be killed.

They changed their minds the very next day.

Chapter Three

It was another glorious spring day.

It is almost impossible for the country-dweller to understand what such a day can mean to the person living in the city. The city citizen has avidly listened to the television weather reports the night before, and now the first thing he does when he awakens to the jangling of the alarm clock is to walk warily to the window and peer up at the sky. He feels a first real awakening thrill if the sky is blue. He knows immediately that this is going to be a day when nothing can go wrong, and then – winter or summer, spring or fall – he will open the window to test the temperature of the air, basing his wardrobe, his attitude, his entire philosophy of life, on the findings he makes in those few first wakeful moments.

Randolph Norden heard the clock-radio go on at 7.30 a.m. He had bought the clock-radio because he figured it would be nice to awaken to music each morning. But his usual rising time was 7.30, news time, and each and every morning he was awakened by the sound of an announcer giving the latest bad news about Russia. He had tried setting the clock-radio for 7.35, at which time the news had given way to music, but he found that he needed those extra five minutes if he was to get to the office on time. He had also tried setting the clock-radio for 7.25, but then he began resenting the loss of five minutes' sleep. And so, each morning, Randolph Norden listened to the bad news on a clock-radio he had bought to provide music. It was, to his way of thinking, another example of the unfairness of life.

As he got out of bed, he heard the announcer telling him about some offshore islands someplace, and he muttered 'Go to hell, you *and* your islands,' and then walked wearily to the bedroom window, pulling up his pyjama top and scratching his belly, generally resenting the clock-radio and his wife, Mae, who was sound asleep in the bed, and even his children who were sound asleep in their separate rooms at the other end of the apartment, and also the maid who, although he was her employer, slept later than he each morning, making it necessary for him to get his own breakfast. He pulled up the shade, feeling reckless as he hoped sunlight would hit the bed and the face of his wife, and then feeling immediately guilty and turning rapidly to see if sunlight had indeed touched Mae's face. It had not. For a desperate moment, he thought, *No sun today,* but then he looked out and over the rooftops to where the sky curved in robin's egg-blue artificiality, and a smile touched his mouth, and he gave a short affirmative nod, and then opened the window.

He stuck his head outside. The air was warm, with a gentle balmy breeze blowing south off the River Harb. From his twelfth-floor apartment, he could see the river traffic and the magnificent span of the bridge in the near distance. The smile widened into a grin. He left the window open, walked back to the bed, turned off the clock-radio, and then took off his pyjamas. He dressed swiftly and soundlessly, putting on underwear, trousers, socks and shoes, and then going into the bathroom where he shaved with an electric razor. As he shaved, his convictions about the day began to take firmer, more confident shape. He was a man who was fond of repeating that his best thoughts always came to him while shaving, and he did indeed have some wonderfully inventive – or so they seemed to him – thoughts while he ran the razor over his stubble. By the time he had finished shaving, put on his shirt, tie and jacket, and had gone into the kitchen to pour himself some juice and brew himself some coffee, he was anxious to get to his law office on Hall Avenue, where he would begin putting some of those wonderfully inventive ideas to work. He gulped his juice and coffee, and then marched to the other end of the apartment, where the children were still in bed. Joanie was awake by now, sitting up and reading a Golden Book, wearing the distorted features of half-asleep awareness.

'G'morning, Daddy,' she said, and then went back to her book.

He kissed her and said, 'I'll see you tonight, huh?' and she nodded and continued reading. He went into the other bedroom, where Mike was still asleep. He did not disturb him. He went, instead, to the other end of the apartment again and kissed Mae, who mumbled something and then rolled over. He smiled, went to the front door, picked up his attaché case, and stepped into the hallway.

The elevator operator said, 'Good morning, Mr Norden. Beautiful day today.'

'Yes, it is, George,' he answered.

They rode in silence to the lobby. He got out, nodded in answer to George's 'Have a good day, Mr Norden,' and then walked to the mailboxes, which he checked routinely even though he knew it was too early for a mail delivery. He opened the front door of the building, stepped out onto the pavement, looked up at the sky, and grinned again.

He was taking a deep breath of fresh spring air when the bullet struck him between the eyes and killed him.

*

The detective who caught the squeal at the 65th Precinct was a fairly hip organization man who tried to keep up with anything important happening in the department. Homicide was a rare and unusual occurrence in the posh 65th, and he was somewhat surprised when the beat patrolman called it in. He put on his hat, motioned to his partner, checked out a police sedan with two bald front tyres, and drove over to where Randolph Norden was lying dead on the sidewalk. It didn't take him very long to realize that Norden had been shot from somewhere high up in one of the buildings across the street, either a window or a roof; the entrance hole was between Norden's eyes, and the exit hole was low on the back of his neck, indicating a very sharp angle of trajectory. He was not a cop anxious to shirk work; he was, in fact, a little reluctant to let go of a bona-fide murder in a precinct where the biggest crimes were usually burglaries or street muggings. But he had read the morning's newspaper, and he knew that a man named Anthony Forrest had been shot to death on Culver Avenue in the eight-seven the day before, and his mind made an automatic connexion – but still, he decided to wait before relinquishing the case. He did not have to wait long.

Ballistics told him that the bullet which had passed through Norden's head and flattened itself against the pavement, and the discharged shell found on the roof of the building across the street, were separate parts of a .308-calibre Remington cartridge. The report went on to point out that the .308 had a full metal case, with a copper-jacketed bullet that had six lands and grooves, a soft point, a right twist, and weighed 191·6 grains. And then, because someone at Ballistics was on the ball, there was an additional hand-written note on the bottom of the report:

Better call Detective 2nd/grade Stephen Carella, 87th Squad, Frederick 7-8024. Investigating similar shooting yesterday; identical cartridge, identical M.O.

G. L.

The detective at the 65th read the report and the additional comment, and then said to no one in particular in the squad-room, 'What the hell makes him think he had to tell me?'

He moved the phone into position and began dialling.

*

The possibility that Carella and Meyer had fastidiously avoided was the possibility that Anthony Forrest had been killed by a sniper.

The sniper is usually a rare breed of murderer who is related to his wartime counterpart only in the methods both employ. The wartime sniper and the peacetime sniper both are hidden, both wait in ambush for their prey. Their success is based on the element of surprise, in combination with a swiftness of action and an accuracy that must be unerring. A wartime sniper hidden in the trees can effectively debilitate and cripple an entire squad, killing several members of it before the squad disperses for cover, pinning down the rest in helpless immobilization. A team of good snipers working in concert can change the outcome of a battle. They are fearful enemies because they rain sudden death from the skies, like the angry wrath of God.

Wartime snipers are trained to kill enemy soldiers. If they kill enough of them, they get medals. A good wartime sniper can even earn the grudging admiration of the men he is trying to kill. They will play a silent game of wits with him, trying to find out where he is, and then trying to discover how they can dislodge him from his vantage-point before he slaughters them all. A wartime sniper is a dangerous expert.

A peacetime sniper is anything.

He can be a kid trying out his new BB gun by taking potshots at passers-by from his bedroom window. He can be a man who shoots at anything wearing red. He can be a Jack the Ripper type who fires at any shapely blonde who passes. He can be an anti-cleric, an anti-vegetarian, an anti-octogenarian, an anti-Semite, an anti-pacifist, an anti-any-human-being. The one clear fact about a peacetime sniper would seem to be that he is anti. And yet the police have often arrested snipers who were shooting people for fun, who had disconnected the act of murder from what they considered to be the sport of shooting. To many snipers, the deadly game is only target practice. To others, it is a hunt, and they will sit in ambush the way some men will sit in a duck blind. To some, it is a form of sexual release. The wartime sniper has a reason and a purpose; the peacetime sniper will most often have neither. The wartime sniper is usually pinned to one spot, lashed to a tree, crowded into a bombed-out attic room. If he moves, he will be spotted and hunted down. Lack of mobility is his tactical weakness. The peacetime sniper can shoot and then vanish. He can do this because his victims are almost always unarmed and never expecting violence. Confusion will generally follow the shooting, and in the confusion he will disappear. There is no one to shoot back at him. He has left a dead man, and now he can take a casual stroll like anyone else in the city.

War is dishonourable, but wartime snipers are only trained technicians doing a job.

Peacetime snipers are wholesale murderers.

Neither Carella nor Meyer wanted their man to be a sniper. The 87th Squad had caught the original squeal, which made the case theirs, a nice, fat, snarling baby left in a basket on the door-step. If their man *was* a sniper, and if he decided to shoot up the entire city, the case was *still* theirs. Oh, yes, there would be additional detectives assigned from other precincts – maybe – and the department would offer whatever help it could – maybe – but the sniper was theirs, and there were ten million people in the city, and any one of them could be either the murderer or the next victim.

How do you play a game without rules?

How do you apply logic to something illogical?

You try.

You start from the beginning.

*

'*If* he's a sniper,' Meyer said. 'We're not even sure of that yet. There've only been two so far, Steve. You want my opinion, I think this guy at the Sixty-fifth – what's his name?'

'Di Nobile.'

'Yeah, I think he dumped this into our laps prematurely.'

'Same m.o.,' Carella said.

'Yeah, yeah.'

'Same cartridge.'

'All men are bipeds,' Meyer said cryptically, 'therefore, all bipeds are men.'

'So?' Carella said.

'So it may be too early to assume that because two guys were shot from two different rooftops, and the same kind of slug was used in both cases, that ...'

'Meyer, I wish to God these guys were both shot by my Aunt Matilda because she's named in their insurance policies as beneficiary. It doesn't look that way so far. So far, there's a pattern.'

'What pattern?'

'The obvious one, to begin with. The way it was done, and the weapon used.'

'Could be a coincidence.'

'Could be, I'll grant you that. But the rest seems to add up.'

'It's too early for anything to be adding up,' Meyer said.

'Yeah? Then try this.' Carella picked up a typewritten sheet from his desk. He glanced up at Meyer once, and then began reading. 'Anthony Forrest was almost forty-five years old, married, with three children. Held an important position, vice-president, salary forty-seven thousand dollars a year. Religion Protestant, politics Republican. You got that?'

'Go ahead.'

'Randolph Norden was forty-six years old, married, with two children. Held an important position, junior partner in a law firm, salary fifty-eight thousand dollars a year. Religion Protestant, politics Republican.'

'So?'

'So change their names, and they could almost be the same guy.'

'Are you trying to tell me you think a sniper is after all middle-aged men who are married, with children, and holding important . . .'

'Maybe.'

'Why not carry it further and isolate some of the facts then?' Meyer said. 'Why don't we simply say our sniper is after anybody in this city who is more than forty-five years old?'

'He might be.'

'Or maybe all married men with a couple or more children, huh?'

'Maybe.'

'Or maybe anybody who earns more than forty thousand a year, huh?'

'Maybe.'

'Or all Protestants? Or all Republicans?'

Carella dropped the typewritten sheet on the desk and said, 'Or maybe only people who have *all* those characteristics.'

'Steve, I imagine that description would fit at least – at the *very* least – a hundred thousand people in this city.'

'So? Who says our sniper hasn't got all the time in the world? He just may be out to get each and every one of them.'

'Then that makes him a nut,' Meyer said.

Carella stared at him. 'Meyer,' he said, 'that's exactly why I was hoping this wouldn't turn out to be a sniper.'

'It isn't yet,' Meyer said. 'Just 'cause that guy from the Sixty-fifth jumps the gun . . .'

'I don't think he jumped the gun. I think he was a smart cop who made the only logical deduction. I think this *is* a sniper, and I *hope* it isn't a nut, and I think we'd better start tracking down both Forrest and Norden to find out what other similarities existed or did not exist. That's what I think.'

Meyer shrugged and then put his hands in his pockets and said, 'All we needed right now was a sniper.'

Chapter Four

The president of Indian Exports, Inc., the firm with which Anthony Forrest had been connected, was a balding man in his sixties, somewhat stout, somewhat pompous, somewhat German. He was perhaps five feet eight inches tall, with a protruding middle and a flat-footed walk. Meyer Meyer, who was Jewish, felt instantly uncomfortable in his presence.

The man's name was Ludwig Etterman. He stood before his desk in what seemed to be genuine despair and he said, with only the faintest German accent, 'Tony was a good man. I cannot understand why this happened.'

'How long had you been associated with him, Mr Etterman?' Carella asked.

'Fifteen years. That is a long time.'

'Can you give us some of the details, sir?'

'What would you like to know?'

'How you met, what sort of business arrangement you had, what Mr Forrest's function was.'

'He was a salesman when we met. I already had the business. He sold cartons for a company that was downtown at the time, it has since gone out of business. We import from India, you know, and we ship goods all over the United States, so naturally we need cartons in which to ship them. At that time, I bought most of my cartons from Tony's company. I saw him, oh, perhaps twice a month.'

'This was shortly after the war, is that right, sir?'

'Yes.'

'Would you know if Mr Forrest had been in the service?'

'Yes, he was,' Etterman said. 'He was with the artillery. He was wounded in Italy, in a battle with the Germans.' Etterman paused. He turned to Meyer and said, 'I am an American citizen, you know. I was here from nineteen twelve, my parents came here when I was still a boy. Most of the family left Germany. Some of them went to India, which is how the business started.'

'Do you know what rank Mr Forrest held in the army, sir?' Carella asked.

'He was a captain, I believe.'

'All right, go ahead, please.'

'Well, I liked him from the beginning. There was a nice manner about him. Cartons, after all, are the same no matter where you buy them. I bought from Tony because I liked him personally.' Etterman offered the detectives a cigar, and then lighted one himself. 'My one vice,' he said. 'My doctor says they will kill me. I told my doctor, I would like to die in bed with a young blonde, or else smoking a cigar.' Etterman chuckled. 'At my age, I will have to be content to die smoking a cigar.'

'How did Mr Forrest come to the firm?' Carella said, smiling.

'I asked him one day if he was satisfied with his position, because if he wasn't I was ready to make him an offer. We discussed it further, and he came to work for the company. As a salesman. That was fifteen years ago. Today, or rather when he died, he was a vice-president.'

'What prompted your offer, Mr Etterman?'

'As I told you, I liked him from the beginning. Then, too ...' Etterman shook his head. 'Well, it does not matter.'

'What, sir?'

'You see ...' Etterman shook his head again. 'You see, gentlemen, I lost my son. He was killed in the war.'

'I'm sorry to hear that,' Carella said.

'Yes, well, it was a long time ago, we must go on living, isn't that so?' He smiled a brief, sad smile. 'He was with a bomber squadron, my son. His plane was shot down in the raid on Schweinfurt on April thirteenth, nineteen forty-four. It was a ball-bearings factory there.'

The room went silent.

'Our family came originally from a town close to Schweinfurt. It is sometimes odd, don't you think, the way life works out? I was born as a German in a town near Schweinfurt, and my son is killed as an American flying over Schweinfurt.' He shook his head. 'It sometimes makes me wonder.'

Again there was silence.

Carella cleared his throat and said, 'Mr Etterman, what sort of a person was Anthony Forrest? Did he get along well with your staff, did he . . .'

'He was the finest human being I have ever known,' Etterman said. 'I do not know of anyone who disliked him.' He shook his head. 'I can only believe that some maniac killed him.'

'Mr Etterman, did he usually leave the office at the same time each day?'

'We close at five,' Etterman said. 'Tony and I would usually talk for, oh, perhaps another fifteen minutes. Yes, I would say he usually left the building between five-fifteen and five-thirty.'

'Did he get along with his wife?'

'He and Clara were very happily married.'

'How about the children? His daughter is nineteen, is that right, and the two boys are about fifteen?'

'That is correct.'

'Any trouble with them?'

'What do you mean?'

'Well, have they ever been in any kind of trouble?'

'I do not know what you mean.'

'With the law, with other kids, bad company, anything like that.'

'They are fine children,' Etterman said. 'Cynthia was graduated highest in her class from high school, and won a scholarship to Ramsey University. The two boys do very well scholastically. One of them is on his school baseball team, and the other belongs to the debating club. No, there was never any trouble with Tony's children.'

'Do you know anything about his army background, Mr Etterman? Whoever shot him is an expert with a rifle, so the possibility that he's an ex-army man exists. Since Mr Forrest *was* in the army . . .'

'I don't know much about it. I'm sure he was a fine officer.'

'He never mentioned having any trouble with his men, anything that might have carried over into . . .'

'Gentlemen, he was in the army during the *war*. The war has been over for a long time. Surely, no one would carry a grudge for so many years.'

'Anything's possible,' Carella said. 'We're looking for a place to hang our hats, sir.'

'It must be a maniac,' Etterman said. 'It can only be a maniac.'

'I hope not, sir,' Carella said, and then they rose and thanked him for his time.

*

On the street outside, Meyer said, 'I always feel funny when I'm around Germans.'

'I noticed that,' Carella said.

'Yeah? Was it really noticeable? Was I too quiet?'

'You didn't say a word all the while we were up there.'

Meyer nodded. 'I kept thinking, "All right, maybe your son was killed flying an American bomber over Schweinfurt, but maybe on the other hand one of your nephews was stuffing my relatives into ovens at Dachau."' Meyer shook his head. 'You know, Sarah and I were at a party a couple of weeks ago, and somebody there was arguing with somebody else because he was selling German cars in this country. What it got down to, the guy said that he would like to see all the German people exterminated. So the other guy said, "There was a German once who wanted to see all the *Jewish* people exterminated." And I could see his point. What the hell makes it more right for Jews to exterminate Germans than vice versa? I could understand the point completely. But at the same time, Steve, something inside me *agreed* with the first guy. Because, I guess maybe deep down inside, every Jew in the world would like to see the Germans exterminated for what they did to us.'

'You can't hate a people here and now for what another people in another time did, Meyer,' Carella said.

'You're not a Jew,' Meyer said.

'No, I'm not. But I look at a guy like Etterman, and I see only a sad old man who lost his son in the war, and who two days ago lost the equivalent of a second son.'

'I look at him, and I see the film clips of those bulldozers pushing thousands of dead Jews, that's what I see.'

'Do you see the son who died over Schweinfurt?'

'No. I think I honestly hate the Germans, and I think I'll hate them till the day I die.'

'Maybe you're entitled to,' Carella said.

'You know, there are times when I think you're Jewish,' Meyer answered.

'When I think of what happened in Germany, I *am* Jewish,' Carella said. 'How can I be anything else and still call myself a human being? What the hell were they throwing in those ovens? Garbage? Animals? Don't you think I feel what you feel?'

'I'm not sure you do,' Meyer said.

'No? Then go to hell.'

'You getting sore or something?'

'A little.'

'Why?'

'I'll tell you why. I don't think I even knew a Jew until I was twelve years old. That's the God's honest truth. Oh yeah, there was a guy who used to come around to the door selling stuff, and my mother called him "The Jew". She used to say, "The Jew is coming today." I don't think she meant anything derogatory, or maybe she did, who the hell knows? She was raised in Italy, and she didn't know Jews from a hole in the wall. Maybe, for her, "Jew" was synonymous with pedlar. To me, a Jew was an old man with a beard and a bundle on his back. Until I got to high school. That was where I met Jews for the first time. You have to remember that Hitler was already in power by then. Well, I heard a joke one day, and I repeated it to a Jewish kid in the cafeteria. The joke was built on a riddle, and the riddle was: "What's the fastest thing in the world?" The answer was: "A Jew riding through Germany on a bicycle." The kid I told the joke to didn't think it was very funny. I couldn't understand what I'd said to offend him. So I went home and asked my father, who was also born in Italy, who was running a bakery, well, you know, he still does. I told him the joke, and he didn't laugh either, and then he took me inside, we had a dining-room at the time with one of those big old mahogany tables. We sat at the table, and he said to me in Italian, "Son, there is nothing good about hatred, and nothing funny about it, either." I went back to school the next day, and I looked for that kid, I can still remember his name, Reuben Zimmerman, and I told him I was sorry for what I'd said the day before, and he told me to forget it. But he never spoke to me again all the while we were in that high school. Four years, Meyer, and he never spoke to me.'

'What are you saying, Steve?'

'I don't know what the hell I'm saying.'

'Maybe you are Jewish, after all,' Meyer said.

'Maybe I am. Let's stop for an egg cream before we look up Norden's wife.'

*

Mae Norden was forty-three years old, a brunette with a round face and dark-brown eyes. They found her at the funeral home where Norden's body lay in a satin-lined coffin. The undertaker had done a remarkable job with the front of his face where the bullet had entered. The casual observer would never have known he'd been shot. The room was filled with relatives and friends, among whom were his wife and his two children, Joanie and Mike. Mike was eight years old and Joanie was five. They both sat on straightbacked chairs near the coffin looking very old and very bewildered at the same time. Mae Norden was dressed in black, and her eyes looked as if she had cried a lot in the past day, but she was not crying now. She led the detectives outside, and they stood on the sidewalk there and smoked cigarettes and discussed her husband who lay dead on satin in the silent room beyond.

'I don't know who could have done this,' Mae said. 'I know it's common for a wife to think her husband was well-liked, but I can't think of a single person who disliked Randy. That's the truth.'

'How about business associates, Mrs Norden? He was a lawyer, isn't that right?'

'Yes.'

'Is it possible that one of his clients ...?'

'Look, anyone who shoots someone has to be a little crazy, isn't that so?'

'Not necessarily,' Meyer said.

'My point is, sure, Randy lost cases. Is there a lawyer who doesn't lose cases? But if you ask me whether or not any of his clients would be ... be angry enough to do something like this, then I have to say how do I know what a crazy person would do?

Where's the basis for ... for *anything* when you're dealing with someone who's unbalanced?'

'We're not sure the killer was unbalanced, Mrs Norden,' Meyer said.

'No?' She smiled thinly. 'A perfectly normal person went up on that roof and shot my husband when he came out of the building, is that it? Perfectly sane?'

'Mrs Norden, we're not psychiatrists. We're talking about sanity in the eyes of the law. The murderer may not have been what the law considers insane.'

'The hell with the law,' Mae said suddenly. 'Anyone who takes another man's life is insane, and I don't care *what* the law says.'

'But your husband was a lawyer, isn't that right?'

'That's exactly right,' Mae said angrily. 'What are you saying now? That I have no respect for the law, therefore I have no respect for lawyers, therefore I have ...'

'We didn't say that, Mrs Norden.' Carella paused. 'I feel certain a lawyer's wife would have a great deal of respect for the law.'

'But I'm not a lawyer's wife any more,' Mae said, 'didn't you know that? I'm a widow. I'm a widow with two young children, Mr – what was your name?'

'Carella.'

'Yes. I'm a forty-three-year-old widow, Mr Carella. Not a lawyer's wife.'

'Mrs Norden, perhaps you can tell us a few things that might help us to find the man who killed your husband.'

'Like what?'

'Did he usually leave the apartment at the same time each morning?'

'Yes. On weekdays. On Saturdays and Sundays, he slept late.'

'Then anyone who had made a habit of observing him would know that he went to work at the same time each day?'

'I suppose so.'

'Mrs Norden, was your husband a veteran?'

'A veteran? You mean, was he in the service?'

'Yes.'

'He was in the navy for three years during World War Two,' Mae said.

'The navy. Not the army.'

'The navy, yes.'

'He was a junior partner in his firm, is that correct?'

'Yes.'

'How did he feel about that?'

'Fine. How should he have felt about it?'

'How many partners were there, Mrs Norden?'

'Three, including my husband.'

'Was your husband the only junior partner?'

'Yes. He was the youngest man in the firm.'

'Did he get along with the others?'

'Very well. He got along with everyone. I just told you that.'

'No trouble with any of the partners, right?'

'That's right.'

'What sort of law did he practise?'

'The firm handled every kind of case.'

'Criminal?'

'Sometimes.'

'Did your husband ever represent a criminal?'

'Yes.'

'How many?'

'Three or four, I don't remember. Four, I guess, since he's been with the firm.'

'Acquittals or convictions?'

'Two of his clients were convicted, two were acquitted.'

'Where are the convicted men now?'

'Serving jail sentences, I would imagine.'

'Would you remember their names?'

'No. But Sam could probably ... Sam Gottlieb, one of the partners. He would know.'

'Was your husband a native of this city, Mrs Norden?'

'Yes. He went through the city school system, and also college and law school here.'

'Where?'

'Ramsey.'

'And how did you come to know him?'

'We met in Grover Park one day. At the zoo. We began seeing each other regularly, and eventually we were married.'

'Before he went into the service, or afterwards?'

'We were married in nineteen forty-nine.'

'Had you known him while he was in the service?'

'No. He went into the navy immediately after graduation. He took his bar exams as soon as he was discharged. He passed them and began practising shortly afterwards. When I met him, he had his own small office in Bethtown. He didn't move to Gottlieb and Graham until three years ago.'

'He had his own practice up to that time?'

'No. He'd been with several firms over the years.'

'Any trouble anywhere?'

'None.'

'Criminal cases at those firms, too?'

'Yes, but I can hardly remember what ...'

'Can you tell us which firms those were, Mrs Norden?'

'You don't really believe this can be someone he lost a case for, do you?'

'We don't know, Mrs Norden. Right now, we have almost nothing to go on. We're trying to find something, anything.'

'I'll write out a list for you,' she said. 'Will you come inside, please?' In the doorway of the funeral home, she stopped and said, 'Forgive me if I was rude to you.' She paused. 'I loved my husband very much, you see.'

Chapter Five

On Monday, April 30, five days after the first murder had been committed, Cynthia Forrest came to see Steve Carella. She walked up the low flat steps at the front of the grey precinct building, past the green globes lettered with the white numerals *87*, and then into the muster room where a sign told her she must state her business at the desk. She told Sergeant Murchison she wanted to talk to Detective Carella, and Murchison asked her her name, and she said, 'Cynthia Forrest', and he rang Carella upstairs, and then told her to go on up. She followed the white sign that read DETECTIVE DIVISION and climbed the iron-runged steps to the second floor of the building, coming out onto a narrow corridor. She followed the corridor past a man in a purple sports shirt who was handcuffed to a bench, and then paused at the slatted wood railing, standing on tiptoes, searching. When she spotted Carella rising from his desk to come to her, she impulsively raised her arm and waved at him.

'Hello, Miss Forrest,' he said, smiling. 'Come on in.' He held open the gate in the railing, and then led her to his desk. She was wearing a white sweater and a dark-grey skirt. Her hair was hemp-coloured, long, pulled to the back of her head in a pony tail. She was carrying a notebook and some texts, and she put these on his desk, sat, crossed her legs, and pulled her skirt down over her knees.

'Would you like some coffee?' Carella asked.

'Is there some?'

'Sure. Miscolo!' he yelled. 'Can we get two cups of joe?'

From the depths of the Clerical Office in the corridor, Miscolo's voice bellowed, 'Coming!'

Carella smiled at the girl and said, 'What can I do for you, Miss Forrest?'

'Most everyone calls me Cindy,' she said.

'All right. Cindy.'

'So this is where you work.'

'Yes.'

'Do you like it?'

Carella looked around the room as if discovering it for the first time. He shrugged. 'The office, or what I do?' he asked.

'Both.'

'The office . . .' He shrugged again. 'I guess it's a rat-trap, but I'm used to it. The work? Yes, I enjoy it, or I wouldn't do it.'

'One of my psych instructors said that men who choose violent professions are usually men of violence.'

'Oh?'

'Yes,' Cindy said. She smiled faintly, as though enjoying a secret joke. 'You don't look very violent.'

'I'm not. I'm a very gentle soul.'

'Then my psych instructor is wrong.'

'I may be the exception that proves the rule.'

'Maybe.'

'Are you a psych major?' Carella asked.

'No. I'm studying to be a teacher. But I'm taking general psych and abnormal psych. And then later, I'll have to take all the educational psychology courses, ed psych one and two and . . .'

'You've got your work cut out for you,' Carella said.

'I suppose so.'

'What do you want to teach?'

'English.'

'College?'

'High school.'

Miscolo came in from the Clerical Office and placed two cups of coffee on Carella's desk. 'I put sugar and milk in both of them, is that all right?' he asked.

'Cindy?'

'That's fine.' She smiled graciously at Miscolo. 'Thank you.'

'You're welcome, miss,' Miscolo said, and went back to his office.

'He seems very sweet,' Cindy said.

Carella shook his head. 'A violent man. Terrible temper.'

Cindy laughed, picked up her coffee-cup, and sipped at it. She put the cup down, reached into her handbag for a package of cigarettes, was about to put one in her mouth, when she stopped and asked, 'Is it all right to smoke?'

'Sure,' Carella said. He struck a match for her, and held it to the cigarette.

'Thank you.' She took several drags, sipped more coffee, looked around the room a little, and then turned back towards Carella, smiling. 'I like your office,' she said.

'Well, good. I'm glad.' He paused, and then asked, 'What did you have on your mind, Cindy?'

'Well . . .' She dragged on the cigarette again, smoking the way a very young girl smokes, a little too feverishly, with too much obvious enjoyment, and yet at the same time with too much casualness. 'They buried Daddy on Saturday, you know.'

'I know.'

'And I read in the newspapers that another man was killed.'

'That's right.'

'Do you think the same person did it?'

'We don't know.'

'Do you have any ideas yet?'

'Well, we're working on it,' Carella said.

'I asked my abnormal-psych instructor what he knew about snipers,' Cindy said, and paused. 'This *is* a sniper, isn't it?'

'Possibly. What did your instructor say?'

'He said he hadn't read very much about them, and didn't even know whether or not any studies had been done. But he had some ideas.'

'Yes? Like what?'

'He felt that the sniper was very much like the peeper. The Peeping Tom, do you know?'

'Yes?'

'Yes. He thought the dynamic was essentially the same.'

'And what was that? The dynamic?'

'A response to infantile glimpses of the primal scene,' Cindy said.

'The primal scene?'

'Yes.'

'What's the primal scene?' Carella asked innocently.

Unflinchingly, Cindy replied, 'The parents having intercourse.'

'Oh. Oh, I see.'

'My instructor said that every child watches and attempts to pretend he is not watching. The sniper comes equipped with an obvious symbol, the rifle, and usually makes use of a telescopic sight, repeating the furtive way things are carried out in childhood, the looking and not being seen, the doing and not being caught.'

'I see,' Carella said.

'Essentially, my instructor said, sniping is a sexually aggressive act. Witnessing of the primal scene can manifest itself neurotically either through peeping – the *voyeur* – or through the reverse of peeping, in effect a fear of being peeped *at*. But the dynamic remains essentially the same with both the peeper and the sniper. Both are hidden, furtive, surreptitious. Both find sexual stimulation, and often gratification, in the act.' Cindy put out her cigarette, stared at Carella with wide, young, innocent blue eyes and said, 'What do you think?'

'Well – I don't know,' Carella said.

'Doesn't the department have a psychologist?' Cindy asked.

'Yes, it does.'

'Why don't you ask him what he thinks?'

'They only do that on television,' Carella said.

'Isn't it important for you to know what's motivating the killer?'

'Yes, certainly. But motives are often very complex things. Your abnormal-psychology instructor may be absolutely correct about an individual sniper, or maybe even ten thousand snipers, but it's possible we'll run into ten thousand others who never witnessed the – primal scene, did you call it? – and who ...'

'Yes, primal scene. But isn't that unlikely?'

'Nothing's unlikely in murder,' Carella said.

Cindy raised her eyebrows dubiously. 'That doesn't sound very scientific, you know.'

'It isn't.' He ended the sentence there with no intention of being rude, and then suddenly realized he had sounded rather abrupt.

'I didn't mean to take up your time,' Cindy said, rising, her manner decidedly cool now. 'I simply thought you might like to know ...'

'You haven't finished your coffee,' Carella said.

'Thank you, but it's very bad coffee,' she answered, and she stood and looked down at him with her shoulders back and her eyes blazing a challenge.

'That's right,' Carella said. 'It's very bad coffee.'

'I'm glad we agree on something.'

'I wasn't aware we had *dis*agreed on anything.'

'I was only trying to help, you know.'

'I appreciate that.'

'But I suppose I had the mistaken notion that modern police departments might want to know about the psychological forces at work in the criminal mind. My fantasy . . .'

'Come on,' Carella said. 'You're too nice and too young to be getting sore at a dumb flatfoot.'

'I'm not nice, and I'm not young, and you're not dumb!' Cindy said.

'You're nineteen.'

'I'll be twenty in June.'

'Why do you say you're not nice?'

'Because I've seen too much and heard too much.'

'Like what?'

'Nothing!' she snapped.

'I'm interested, Cindy.'

Cindy picked up her books and held them clasped to her breast. 'Mr Carella, this isn't the Victorian Age. Just remember that.'

'I'll try to. But suppose you tell me what you mean.'

'I mean that most seventeen-year-olds today have seen and heard everything there is to see or hear.'

'How dull that must be,' Carella said. 'What do you do when you're eighteen? Or nineteen?'

'When you're nineteen,' Cindy said in an icy voice, 'you go looking for the cop who first told you your father was dead. You go looking for him in the hope you can tell him something he might not know, something to help him. And then, the way it always is with so-called adults, you're completely disappointed when you discover he won't even listen.'

'Sit down, Cindy. What did you want to tell me about our sniper? If he *is* a sniper, to begin with.'

'A man who shoots at someone from a rooftop is certainly . . .'

'Not necessarily.'

'He killed two men in the same way!'

'*If* he's the one who killed both men.'

'The newspaper said the same make and calibre of cartridge . . .'

'That could mean a lot, or could mean nothing.'

'You're not seriously telling me you think it was a coincidence?'

'I don't know what to tell you, except that we're considering every possibility. Sit down, will you? You make me nervous.'

Cindy sat down abruptly and plunked her books on the desktop. For a nineteen-year-old who had seen and heard all there was to see and hear, she looked very much like a nine-year-old at that moment.

'Well,' Cindy said, '*if* the same man killed my father and that other man, and *if* he's a sniper, then I think you ought to consider the possibility that he may be sexually motivated.'

'We will indeed.'

Cindy rose abruptly and began picking up her books. 'You're having me on, Detective Carella,' she said, angrily, 'and I don't particularly like it!'

'I'm not having you on! I'm listening to every word you're saying, but for God's sake, Cindy, don't you think we've ever dealt with snipers before?'

'What?'

'I said don't you think the police department has ever handled a case involving –'

'Oh.' Cindy put her books down again, and again she sat in the chair alongside his desk. 'I never thought of that. I'm sorry.'

'That's all right.'

'I'm truly sorry. Of course. I mean, I suppose you run across all sorts of things. I'm terribly sorry.'

'I'm glad you came up anyway, Cindy.'

'Are you?' Cindy asked suddenly.

'We don't often get nice bright kids in here,' Carella said. 'It's a refreshing change, believe me.'

'I'm just the all-American girl, huh?' Cindy said, with a

peculiar smile. Then she rose, shook hands with Carella, thanked him, and left.

*

The woman walking along Culver Avenue was neither a nice bright kid nor an all-American girl.

She was forty-one years old, and her hair was bleached a bright blonde, and she wore too much lipstick on her mouth and too much rouge on her cheeks. Her skirt was black and tight, and dusted with powder she had spilled on it while making up her face. She wore a high brassiere and a tight, white, soiled sweater, and she carried a black patent-leather handbag, and she looked very much like a prostitute, which is exactly what she was.

In a day and age when prostitutes in any neighbourhood look more like high-fashion models than ladies of the trade, the woman's appearance was startling, if not contradictory. It was almost as if, by so blatantly announcing her calling, she were actually denying it. Her clothes, her posture, her walk, her fixed smile all proclaimed – as effectively as if the words had been lettered on a sandwich board – I AM A PROSTITUTE. But as the woman walked past, the imaginary back of the sandwich board was revealed, and lettered there in scarlet letters – what else? – were the words: I AM DIRTY! DO NOT TOUCH!

The woman had had a rough day. In addition to being a prostitute, or perhaps *because* she was a prostitute, or perhaps she was a prostitute because of *it* – God, there are so many psychological complexes to consider these days – the woman was also a drunk. She had awakened at 6 a.m. with bats and mice crawling out of the plaster cracks in her cheap furnished room, and she had discovered there was no more booze in the bottle beside her bed, and she had swiftly dressed, swiftly because she rarely wore anything but a bra under her street clothes, and taken to the streets. By twelve noon, she had raised the price of a bottle of cheap whisky, and by 1 p.m. she had downed the last drop. She had awakened at 4 p.m. to find the bats and mice crawling out of the cracks again and to find, again, that the bottle beside the bed was empty. She had put on her bra and sweater, her black skirt and her high-heeled black pumps; she had dusted her face with powder, smeared lipstick on her mouth and rouge on her cheeks, and now she was walking along a familiar stretch of avenue as dusk settled in the sky to the west.

She generally walked this pavement each night along about dusk, drunk or sober, because there was a factory on Culver and North Fourteenth, and the men from the factory quit at five-thirty, and sometimes she was lucky enough to find a quick four-dollar partner or, if her luck was running exceptionally good, even a partner for the night at fifteen dollars in good, hard, American currency.

Tonight she felt lucky.

Tonight, as she saw the men pouring from the factory on the next corner, she felt certain there would be a winner among them. Maybe even someone who would like to do a little honest drinking before they tumbled into the sack. Maybe someone who would fall madly in love with her, the plant superintendent maybe, or even an executive who would love her eyes and her hair and take her home to his large bachelor house in the suburbs of Larksview, where she would have an upstairs maid and a butler and make love only when she felt like it, don't make me laugh.

Still, she felt lucky.

She was still feeling lucky when the bullet smashed through her upper lip, shattering the gum ridge, careening downwards through her windpipe, cracking her upper spine, and blowing a huge hole out of her neck as it left her body.

The bullet spent itself against the brick wall of the building against which she fell dead.

The bullet was a Remington .308.

Chapter Six

It is true that in a democracy all men are equal in the eyes of the law, but this does not necessarily apply to all *dead* men. It would be nice to believe that a detective investigating the murder of a Skid Row wino devoted all his time and energy to the case in an attempt to discover the perpetrator. It would be nicer to believe that the untimely demise of a numbers runner or a burglar occasioned anything but relief, an attitude of 'Good riddance' on the part of the police. But there is a vast difference between a murdered millionaire and a murdered criminal. A prostitute, who steals nothing, is nonetheless guilty of a violation, and in the lexicon of the police is a criminal. The death of the Culver Avenue prostitute would have caused little more than slight passing interest, had it not been for the fact that she was slain by a .308-calibre Remington cartridge. As it was, she acquired more status in death than she had ever known in life, either in the eyes of men or in the eyes of the law.

The law is curiously ambiguous concerning prostitutes. The Penal Law describes Prostitution and Disorderly Houses in detail, but there is nowhere in the code a definition of a prostitute *per se*. Under the section on Prostitution, there are listed:

(1) Abduction of female for purposes of
(2) Compulsory prostitution of women
(3) Compelling prostitution of wife of another
(4) Corroboration of testimony of female compelled or procured
(5) Pimps and procurers
(6) Transporting women for purposes of

Under the section on Disorderly Houses there are listed:

(1) Abduction of females
(2) Admission of minors

(3) Compulsory prostitution in
(4) Keeping or renting
(5) Sending messenger boys to

... and so on. Some of these crimes are felonies. But nowhere in these subdivisions is there reference to the crime of the prostitute herself. There is only one place in the Penal Law where love for sale is defined. Curiously, it is in Section 722, which defines Disorderly Conduct: 'Any person who with intent to provoke a breach of the peace, or whereby a breach of the peace may be occasioned, commits any of the following acts shall be deemed to have committed the offence of disorderly conduct.'

The 'following acts' include anything from using threatening language, to causing a crowd to collect, to making insulting remarks to passing pedestrians, and – under Subdivision 9: 'Frequents or loiters about any public place soliciting men for the purpose of committing a crime against nature or any other lewdness.'

If one can call going to bed with a man 'a crime against nature', then that is prostitution. It is not called prostitution in this section. It is called 'soliciting', but in the section titled 'Solicitation: Lewd or immoral purposes, solicitation for', there is listed only the following: 'Male persons living on proceeds of prostitution: Every male person who lives wholly or in part on the earnings of prostitution, or who in any public place solicits for immoral purposes, is guilty of a misdemeanour. A male person who lives with or is habitually in the company of a prostitute and has no visible means of support, shall be presumed to be living on the earnings of prostitution.'

So what is an honest, conscientious cop supposed to do when an obvious whore sidles up to him and asks, 'Want some fun, honey?' Left to his own devices, he might accept the offer. Bound by the Penal Law, he might arrest her for disorderly conduct, the penalty for which can be a jail sentence not to exceed six months, or a fine not to exceed fifty dollars, or both. But the Penal Law is bolstered by the Code of Criminal Procedure, and every cop in the city knows Section 887, Subdivision 4, by heart. Every prostitute has committed it to memory, too, because this is where they get her by the codes. Section 887 describes, of all things, vagrants. 'The following persons are vagrants', it states, and then goes on to list everyone including your Uncle Max. When it comes to Subdivision 4, it pulls no punches.

4. A person (a) who offers to commit prostitution, or (b) who offers to secure for another for the purpose of prostitution or for any other lewd or indecent act; or (c) who loiters in or near any thoroughfare or public or private place for the purpose of inducing, enticing or procuring another to commit lewdness, fornication, unlawful sexual intercourse or any other indecent act ...

That would seem to cover it, man. But those puritan forefathers weren't taking any chances. Section 887, Subdivision 4, goes on to state:

... or (d) who in any manner induces, entices or procures a person who is in any thoroughfare or public place or private place, to commit any such acts; or (e) who receives or offers or agrees to receive any person into any place, structure, house, building or conveyance for the purpose of prostitution, lewdness or assignation or knowingly permits any person to remain there for such purposes; or (f) who in any way, aids or abets or participates in the doing of any of the acts or things enumerated in Subdivision four of Section eight hundred and eighty-seven of the Code of Criminal Procedure; or (g) who is a common prostitute, who has no lawful employment whereby to maintain herself.

That's a vagrant, sir, madam. And if that is what you are, you can under Section 891 (a) of the same code be sent to a reformatory for as long as three years, or a county jail, penitentiary or other penal institution for as long as a year – so watch yourself!

The man named Harry Wallach was a male person who lived with or was habitually in the company of the prostitute named Blanche Lettiger, the woman who had been shot to death on the night of April 30. It did not take the police long to find him. Everybody knew who Blanche's 'old man' was. They picked him up the next morning in a poolroom on North Forty-first, and they brought him to the station house and sat him down in a chair and began asking their questions. He was a tall, well-dressed man, with hair greying at the temples, and penetrating green eyes. He asked the detectives if it was all right to smoke, and then he lighted a fifty-cent cigar and sat back calmly with a faint superior smile on his mouth as Carella opened the session.

'What do you do for a living, Wallach?'

'Investment,' Wallach said.

'What kind of investment?' Meyer asked.

'Stocks, bonds, real estate. You know.'

'What's the current quotation on AT&T?' Carella asked.

'Not in my portfolio,' Wallach said.

'What *is* in your portfolio?'

'I don't remember offhand.'

'Do you have a broker?'

'Yes.'

'What's his name?'

'He's in Miami right now on vacation.'

'We didn't ask you where he was, we asked you what his name is.'

'Dave.'

'Dave what?'

'Dave Milias.'

'Where's he staying in Miami?'

'Search me,' Wallach said.

'All right, Wallach,' Meyer said, 'what do you know about this woman Blanche Lettiger?'

'Blanche *who*?' Wallach said.

'Oh, you want to play this one cool, huh, Wallach? Is that it?'

'It's just the name don't seem to ring a bell.'

'It doesn't, huh? Blanche Lettiger. You share an apartment with her on Culver and North Twelfth, apartment 6B, rented under the name of Frank Wallace, and you've been living there with her for the past year and a half. Does the name ring a bell now, Wallach?'

'I don't know what you're talking about,' Wallach said.

'Maybe he's the guy who plugged her, Steve.'

'I'm beginning to think so.'

'What do you mean?' Wallach asked, unruffled.

'Why the dodge, Wallach? You think we're interested in a crummy pimp like you?'

'I'm not that,' Wallach said with dignity.

'No? What do you call it?'

'Not what you said.'

'Oh, how sweet,' Meyer said. 'He doesn't want to spoil his dainty little lips by saying the word *pimp*. Look, Wallach, don't make this hard for us. You want us to throw the book, we've got it, and we know how to throw it. Make it easy for yourself. We're only interested in knowing about the woman.'

'What woman?'

'You son of a bitch, she was shot down in cold blood last night. What the hell are you, a human being or what?'

'I don't know any woman who was shot down in cold blood last night,' Wallach insisted. 'You're not going to get me involved in a goddamn homicide. I know you guys too good. You're looking for a patsy, and it ain't going to be me.'

'We weren't looking for a patsy,' Carella said, 'but now that you mention it, it's not a bad idea. What do you think, Meyer?'

'Why not?' Meyer said. 'He's as good as anybody to pin it on. Take the heat off us.'

'Where were you last night, Wallach?'

'What time last night?' Wallach answered, still calm, still puffing gently on his cigar.

'The time the woman was killed.'

'I don't know what time any woman was killed.'

'About five-thirty. Where were you?'

'Having dinner.'

'So early?'

'I eat early.'

'Where?'

'The Rambler.'

'Where's that?'

'Downtown.'

'Downtown where? Look, Wallach, if you force us to pull teeth, we know some better ways of doing it.'

'Sure, get out your rubber hose,' Wallach said calmly.

'Meyer,' Carella said calmly, 'get the rubber hose.'

Calmly, Meyer walked to a desk on the far side of the room, opened the top drawer, took out a two-foot length of rubber hose, smacked it against his palm, and then walked back to where Wallach was watching him, calmly.

'This what you mean, Wallach?'

'You think you're surprising me or something? Wallach asked.

'Who'd you eat with?' Carella said.

'Alone.'

'We don't need the hose, Meyer. He just cooked his own goose.'

'That's what you think, buddy. The waiter'll remember me.'

'Well, that depends on how much we lean on the waiter, doesn't it?' Carella said. 'We're looking for a patsy, remember? You think we're going to let a lousy waiter stand in our way?'

'He'll say I was there,' Wallach said, but his voice was beginning to lack conviction.

'Well, I certainly hope so,' Carella said. 'But in the meantime, we're going to book you for homicide, Wallach. We won't mention the fact that you're a pimp, of course. We'll save that for the trial. It might impress the hell out of a jury.'

'Listen,' Wallach said.

'Yeah?'

'What do you want from me? I didn't kill her, and you know it.'

'Then who did?'

'How the hell do I know?'

'You know the woman?'

'Of *course* I know her. Come on, willya?'

'You said you didn't.'

'I was kidding around. How did I know you guys were so serious? What's everybody getting so excited about?'

'How long have you known her?'

'About two years.'

'Was she a prostitute when you met her?'

'You getting *me* involved again? I don't know what she worked at. *My* means of earning a living is investment. I *lived* with her, that's all. What she done or didn't do was her business.'

'You didn't know she was a hooker, huh?'

'No.'

'Wallach,' Carella said, 'we're going to take you down and book you for homicide. Because you're lying, you see, and that's very suspicious. So unless we come up with somebody who looks better than you for the rap, you're it. Now do you want to be it, Wallach? Or do you want to start telling the truth, so we'll know you're an upstanding citizen who only happens to be a pimp? What do you say, Wallach?'

Wallach was silent for a long time. Then he said, 'She was a hooker when I met her.'

'Two years ago?'

'Two years ago.'

'When did you see her last?'

'I was out night before last. I didn't go back to the pad at all yesterday. I didn't see her all day.'

'What time did you leave the apartment the night before?'

'Around eight.'

'Where'd you go?'

'Uptown. Riverhead.'

'To do what?'

Wallach sighed. 'There was a crap game, all right?'

'Was Blanche in the apartment when you left?'

'Yeah.'

'Did she say anything to you?'

'No. She was in the other room with a John.'

'You brought him to her?'

'Yeah, yeah,' Wallach said and put his cigar in the ashtray. 'I'm playing ball with you, okay?'

'You're playing ball fine, Wallach. Tell us about Blanche.'

'What do you want to know?'

'How old was she?'

'She said she was thirty-five, but she was really forty-one.'

'What's her background? Where's she from?'

'The Middle West someplace. Oklahoma, Iowa, I don't know. One of those hick joints.'

'When did she come here?'

'Years ago.'

'When, Wallach?'

'Before the war. I don't know the exact date. Listen, if you want her life history, you're barking up the wrong tree. I didn't know her that good.'

'Why'd she come here?'

'To go to school.'

'What kind of school?'

'College, what do you think?'

'Where?'

'Ramsey University.'

'How long did she stay there?'

'I don't know.'

'Did she graduate?'

'I don't know.'

'How'd she get to be a hooker?'

'I don't know.'

'Are her parents living?'

'I don't know.'

'Was she married, divorced, would you know?'

'No.'

'What the hell *do* you know, Wallach?'

'I know she was a broad who was over the hill, and I was taking care of her practically as a charity case, okay? I know she was a goddamn lush, and a pain in the ass, and the best thing that coulda happened to her was to get shot in the head, which is what she got, okay? That's what I know.'

'You're a nice guy, Wallach.'

'Thanks, I'm crazy about you, too. What do you want from me? She'da died in the streets a year ago if I hadn't given her a place to stay. I done an act of kindness.'

'Sure.'

'Yeah, sure. What do you think, she made me a millionaire? Who the hell wanted to bang something looked like her? I used to bring her the dregs, that's all. She's lucky she made enough for room and board. Half the time, she never gave me a cent. She had the dough spent on booze before I reached her, and the booze would be gone, too. You think it was a picnic? Try it sometime.'

'How'd a college girl become a hooker?' Carella asked.

'What are you, a cop or a sociologist? There's more hookers in this town who once went to college than I can count. Call the Vice Squad, they'll tell you.'

'Never mind the Vice Squad,' Meyer said. 'You got any idea who killed her?'

'None.'

'You sound very glad to be rid of her.'

'I am. That don't mean I killed her. Look, you guys know I had nothing to do with this. Why are we wasting each other's time?'

'What's your hurry, Wallach? Another crap game?'

'Sure, I'd tell you about it, wouldn't I?'

'Then take your time. We've got all day.'

'Okay, let's shoot the day. What the hell. It's only the tax-payers' money.'

'You never paid a tax in your life, Wallach.'

'I pay taxes every year,' Wallach said indignantly. 'Both federal *and* state, so don't give me that.'

'What do you list as your occupation?'

'We going to go into that again?'

'No, let's get back to Blanche. Did anyone ever threaten her? Would you know that?'

'How would I know? Johns are all different. Some are like little lost kids with their first broad, and some are tough guys who like to smack a girl around. There's something wrong with a guy who goes to a whore in the first place.'

'He's not a pimp,' Meyer said, 'he's a psychologist.'

'I know whores,' Wallach said simply.

'You don't seem to know a hell of a lot about Blanche Lettiger.'

'I told you everything I know. What more can I say?'

'Tell us about her habits.'

'Like what?'

'Like what time she got up in the morning.'

'The morning? You kidding?'

'All right, what then? The afternoon?'

'She usually woke up about one, two in the afternoon and started looking for a bottle.'

'What time did she wake up the day she was killed?'

Wallach smiled, pointed a chiding finger at Carella, and said, 'Ah-ah. Caught you.'

'Huh?' Carella said.

Still smiling, Wallach said, 'I told you I didn't see her at all yesterday, didn't I?'

'I wasn't trying to trip you, Wallach.'

'There ain't a bull in the world who ain't *always* trying to trip guys like me.'

'Look, Wallach,' Carella said, 'we understand you're just a decent, upright, put-upon citizen, okay? So let's send the violinists home and get down to business. You're beginning to get on my nerves.'

'You don't exactly have a calming effect on me,' Wallach replied.

'What the hell is this?' Meyer said, annoyed. 'A vaudeville routine at the Palace? One more crack out of you, you cheap punk, and I'll bust your head open.'

Wallach opened his mouth and then closed it. He looked at Meyer sourly instead.

'Okay?' Meyer shouted.

'Okay, okay,' Wallach answered, sulking.

'Did she make a habit of leaving the apartment between five and five-thirty every afternoon?'

'Yeah.'

'Where'd she go?'

'There was a factory near by the pad. Sometimes the guys coming out of work were good for a strike.'

'She did this *every* afternoon?'

'Not every afternoon, but often enough. When you're in the shape she was in, you've got to take them where they come.'

'Where's the factory?'

'Culver and North Fourteenth.'

'So then almost every afternoon, sometime between five and five-thirty, she'd leave the apartment and walk up towards the factory, right?'

'Yeah.'

'Who knew this besides you, Wallach?'

'The cop on the beat knew it,' Wallach answered, unable to repress the crack. 'Maybe *he's* the one who put the blocks to her, huh?'

'Look, Wallach . . .'

'All right, all right, I don't know who knew it. The guy who killed her, I guess. Anybody coulda known it. All they had to do was watch.'

'You've been a great help,' Carella said. 'Get the hell out of here.'

'You only ruined my day,' Wallach said.

He rose, dusted cigar ash off his trousers, and was walking

away from the desk when Meyer kicked him square in the behind. Wallach didn't even turn. With great dignity, he walked out of the squad-room.

Chapter Seven

So far, the police had done only one concrete thing towards solving the multiple murders: nothing.

That morning, after Wallach left, they tried to remedy the situation somewhat by putting in a call to Samuel Gottlieb of Gottlieb, Graham and Norden. They asked the senior partner of the firm how many criminal cases Norden had handled since he'd been with them, and he told them there had been a total of four. He promptly furnished them with the names of all four clients, and then broke the list down into those who had been acquitted, and those who had been convicted. They then took the list Mrs Norden had given them, the one containing the names of the various other firms Norden had worked for over the years, and by eleven o'clock they had called each firm and had a further list of twelve convicted criminals who had once been clients of Norden. They sent this list to the city's B.C.I. with a request for the whereabouts of each man, and then checked out a car and drove downtown to Ramsey University where they hoped to learn something, anything, about Blanche Lettiger, the dead prostitute.

The university was in the heart of the city, beginning where Hall Avenue ended, sprawling on the fringes of the Quarter, rubbing elbows with Chinatown. An outdoor art exhibition was in full swing on the bordering side streets. Carella parked the car in a no parking zone, pulled down the sun-visor with its hand-lettered sign advising POLICEMAN ON DUTY CALL, and then walked with Meyer past the canvases lined up on the sidewalk. There seemed to be a predominance of seascapes this year. The smiling perpetrators of all this watery art peered hopefully at each passer-by, trying to look aloof and not too eager, but placed nonetheless in the uncomfortable position of being merchants as well as creators.

Meyer glanced only cursorily at the seascapes, and then stopped before an 'action' painting, the action consisting of several bold black slashes across a field of white, with two red dots in one corner. He nodded mysteriously, and then caught up with Carella.

'What happened to people?' he asked.

'What do you mean?' Carella answered.

'There used to be a time when you looked at a painting, there were people in it. No more. Artists aren't interested in people. They're only interested in "expression". I read about a guy who covers a nude lady with paint, and then she rolls on a canvas, and what comes out is a painting.'

'You're kidding,' Carella said.

'I swear to God,' Meyer said. 'You can see where she rubbed with her leg or her thigh, or whatever. She's like the guy's paint-brush.'

'Does he clean his brushes at the end of the day?'

'I don't know. The article didn't say. It just told about how he worked, and it showed some examples.'

'That's pretty far out, isn't it?'

'No, I think it's a return to tradition.'

'How so?'

'The guy is obviously putting people back into painting.'

'There's the school,' Carella said.

Ramsey University sat on the other side of a small park struck with May sunshine. There were several students sitting on the scattered benches discussing the conjugation of the verb *aimer*, discussing too the theory of ratio-mobility. They glanced up momentarily as Meyer and Carella crossed the park and climbed the steps of the Administration Building. The inside of the building was cool and dim. They stopped a student wearing a white shirt and a loose green sweater, and asked him where the Records Office was.

'What records office?' the student asked.

'Where they keep the records.'

'Records of what? You mean the registrar?'

'We mean records of past students.'

'Alumni, you mean?'

'Well, we're not sure this student ever graduated.'

'Matriculated students, do you mean? Or non-matriculated?'

'We're not sure,' Carella said.

'Day session, or night?' the student asked.

'Well, we're not sure.'

'Which college, would you know that?'

'No,' Carella said.

The student looked at him curiously. 'I'm late for class,' he said at last, and wandered off.

'We get an F,' Meyer said. 'We came to school unprepared.'

'Let's talk to the dean,' Carella said.

'Which dean?' Meyer asked, peering at Carella as the student had done. 'Dean of admissions? Dean of men? Dean of women? Dean Martin?'

'Dean I see you someplace before?' Carella said, and Meyer said, 'Ouch!'

The Dean of Admissions was a nice lady in her early sixties who wore a starched ruffled blouse and a pencil in her hair. Her name was Dean Agnes Moriarty, and when the detectives said they were from the police, she immediately quipped, 'Moriarty, meet Holmes and Watson.'

'Carella and Meyer,' Carella said, smiling.

'What can I do for you, gentlemen?'

'We're interested in whatever information we can get about a woman who was once a student here.'

'When?' Miss Moriarty asked.

'We don't know. Sometime before the war, we believe.'

'When before the war? This university was founded in eighteen forty-two, gentlemen.'

'The girl was forty-one years old when she died,' Meyer said. 'We can assume . . .'

'Died?' Miss Moriarty asked, and she raised her eyebrows slightly.

'Yes, ma'am,' Meyer said. 'She was killed last night.'

'Oh.' Miss Moriarty nodded. 'Then this is serious, isn't it?'

'Yes, ma'am.'

'Oh. Well now, let's see. If she was forty-one years old – most of our students begin at eighteen, which would make this twenty-three years ago. Do you have any idea which college she was enrolled in?'

'No, I'm afraid we haven't.'

'Shall we try the school of liberal arts?'

'We're entirely in your hands, Miss Moriarty,' Carella said.

'Well then, let's see what we can find out, shall we?'

They found out that Blanche Ruth Lettiger had indeed enrolled in the Liberal Arts College of Ramsey University as a speech and dramatics major in 1940; that she had given her age as eighteen at the time, and her home address as Jonesboro, Indiana, a town with a population of 1,973, close to Kokomo. She had listed her temporary address as 1107 Horsely Road, in the Quarter. She had remained at the school for one term only, a matter of five months, and had then dropped out. Her withdrawal was somewhat mysterious since she was an honour student with a 3·8 index, close to the perfect 4·0. Miss Moriarty had no idea where Blanche Lettiger had gone after her drop-out. She had never returned to the school, and had never attempted to contact them in any way.

Carella asked Miss Moriarty if there was anyone at the school now who might remember Blanche Lettiger as a student, and Miss Moriarty promptly took the detectives to Professor Richardson in the speech and dramatics department. Richardson was a thin old man with the manner and bearing of a Shakespearian actor. His voice rolled from his mouth in golden, rounded tones. He spoke forcefully, as though he were trying to give the second balcony its money's worth. Carella was certain every word he projected was heard all the way uptown in the squad-room.

'Blanche Lettiger?' he said. 'Blanche Lettiger?'

He put one slender hand to his leonine head, closing the thumb and forefinger over the bridge of his nose, lost in silent thought. Then he nodded once, looked up and said, 'Yes.'

'You remember her?' Carella asked.

'Yes.' Richardson turned to Miss Moriarty. 'Do you recall the Wig and Buskin Society?'

'I do,' she said.

'Then you must also remember *The Long Voyage Home.*'

'I'm afraid I missed that one,' Miss Moriarty said tactfully. 'The school's drama groups do so *many* shows.'

'Mmm, yes, well,' Richardson said. He turned back to Carella.

'I was faculty adviser of the group for four successive years. Blanche worked with us in that play.'

'*The Long Voyage Home*?'

'Yes. A very nice girl. I remember her very well. *And* the play, too. It was the first production we did in the round. Blanche Lettiger, yes, that's right. She played one of the ... ah ... ladies of easy virtue.'

'What do you mean?' Carella said.

'Well —' Richardson paused, glanced at Miss Moriarty, and then said, 'One of the prostitutes.'

Carella glanced at Meyer, but neither of the detectives said anything.

'She was a very nice child,' Richardson said. 'Rather intense, somewhat brooding, but nice nonetheless. And a very good actress. The play is set in a London waterfront dive, you know, and the girl Blanche played spoke with a Cockney dialect. Blanche mastered the tones and accent almost immediately. A remarkable feat, very. She had an excellent memory, too. She had memorized all of her sides —' Richardson paused here to see whether or not anyone had caught his use of the professional term 'sides' and then, getting no reaction, continued — 'in the first two nights of rehearsal. She had quite the largest female part in the play, you know. Freda. The girl who has the long talk with Olson and then is instrumental in drugging him before he's shanghaied. We did the play in the round, the first time anything of the sort had been tried at this school. We used the school theatre, of course, but we banked rows of rented bleachers on the stage, and the performers worked in the centre of it. Very exciting. In one scene, if you recall the play ...'

'Mr Richardson, I wonder if ...'

'...one of the sailors, Driscoll, is supposed to throw the beer in his glass into the face of Ivan, the drunken Russian sailor. Well, when ...'

'Mr Richardson, do you know if ...'

'... the actor hurled the contents of his glass, he spattered half a dozen people sitting in the first row. The immediacy of playing in the round is difficult to ...'

'Mr Richardson,' Carella said firmly, 'did Blanche Lettiger ...'

'. . . imagine unless you've done it. Blanche was excellent at it. She had a very expressive face, you see. In the scene with Olson, she was required to do a lot of listening, a task even professional actresses find difficult. It was especially difficult here because we were working in the round, where every nuance of expression is clearly visible to the audience. But Blanche carried it off beautifully, a remarkable performance, very.'

'Did she want to . . .'

'The play isn't one of my particular favourites, you know,' Richardson said. 'Of the *Glencairn* series, I much prefer *The Moon of the Caribbees*, or even *In the Zone*. But *Moon of the Caribbees* has four women who are all West Indian Negresses, which would rather have limited our female casting; there are, after all, *white* students to consider, too. *In the Zone*, of course, has an all-male . . .'

'Would you know whether Miss Lettiger . . .'

'. . . cast, and this is, after all, a coeducational institution, so we eliminated that one. As a matter of fact, *The Long Voyage Home*, despite its shortcomings, was extremely well suited to our needs. With the exception of two rather small parts at the very end of the play, the parts are rather well . . .'

'Mr Richardson,' Carella said, 'would you know whether or not Miss Lettiger had any idea of becoming a professional actress? Or was this simply another extra-curricular activity for her?'

'I honestly don't know how serious she was about the theatre. We discussed it peripherally once or twice, but my notion is she was undecided. Or perhaps intimidated, I'm not sure. I think the city overwhelmed her a bit. She was, after all, only eighteen years old, and from a small town in Indiana, very. The notion of attempting to conquer the professional theatre must have seemed extremely far-fetched to her.'

'She *was* a speech and dramatics major, though?'

'Yes. But, of course, she was only here at the school for one term, not even a full semester.'

'Had she spoken to you about leaving school?'

'No.'

'Were you surprised when she left?'

'Mr Canella, the one thing an instructor . . .'

'Carella.'

'Carella, yes, forgive me. The one thing an instructor learns over the years is never to be surprised by anything a student says or does.'

'Does that mean you *were* surprised?'

'Well, she was an excellent student and, as I told you, a talented girl, very. Yes, I suppose I was surprised.'

'Was she in any production besides the O'Neill play?'

'No.'

'Was she in any of your classes?'

'No.'

'Would you know if she had any relatives in this city?'

'I'm sorry, I have no idea.'

'Well, thank you,' Carella said.

'Not at all. My pleasure,' Richardson answered.

They left him in his small office and walked downstairs with Miss Moriarty. 'He's a crashing bore, *very*,' she said, 'but his memory *is* good, and I'm sure he gave an accurate picture of Blanche Lettiger as she was then. Was it at all helpful?'

'Miss Moriarty,' Carella said, 'the terrible thing about detective work is that you never know what's helpful and what isn't until all the pieces fit together at the end.'

'I'll remember that,' Miss Moriarty said. 'It'll no doubt help me in my sworn and unceasing battle against Holmes.'

'May the best man win,' Carella said.

They shook hands with her and walked out into the sunshine again.

'What do you think?' Meyer asked.

'I don't know what to think. Why'd she drop out of school so suddenly? Good student, good marks, interested in extra-curricular stuff,' Carella shrugged.

'It's pretty unusual, isn't it? Especially when she came all the way from Kokomo.'

'No, not Kokomo, some town near it.'

'Yeah, what was the name of that town again?'

'Jonesville, something like that.'

'Jonesboro,' Meyer said.

'That's right.'

'You think we ought to get a flyer out?'

'What for?'

'Routine check on her family, relatives, I don't know.'

'What good would it do? I'll tell you what bugs me about this girl, Meyer. She breaks the pattern, you know? Before, there was at least some kind of slender thread. Now –' He shrugged. 'This bothers me. It really does.'

'Yeah, well you don't see *me* grinning from ear to ear, do you?'

'Maybe we *are* up against a nut. If we are, we can just whistle. He'll shoot whoever the hell he wants to, at random, without rhyme or reason.'

'Who's that blonde waving at you?' Meyer said suddenly.

Carella, who thought Meyer was joking, said, 'Blondes always wave at me.'

'Yeah? Even sixteen-year-old ones?'

Carella followed Meyer's gaze to the other end of the park, where a young blonde girl wearing a navy skirt and a pale-blue sweater had begun walking quickly towards them. He recognized her immediately, and raised his own arm in greeting.

'You know her?' Meyer asked.

'Sure. Part of my fan club.'

'I keep forgetting you're a big-shot city detective.'

'Try to remember, will you?'

Cindy Forrest was wearing her hair loose around her face. There was a trace of lipstick on her mouth, and a string of tiny pearls around her throat. She was carrying her books hugged against her breast, carrying also a small secret smile on her face as she approached.

'Hi,' she said. 'Were you looking for me?'

'No,' Carella answered, 'but it's nice to see you, anyway.'

'Why, thank you, sir,' Cindy said. 'What are you doing all the way down here?'

'Looking up some records. What are *you* doing here?'

'I go to school here,' Cindy said. 'Remember? My abnormal-psych instructor? Witness of the primal scene?'

'I remember,' Carella said. 'You're a psychology major, right?'

'Wrong. I'm an education major.'

'And you want to teach college,' he said, nodding.

'High school,' Cindy corrected.

'Some detective,' Meyer said, sighing.

'Meyer, I'd like you to meet Cynthia Forrest. Miss Forrest, this is my partner, Detective Meyer.'

'How do you do, Mr Meyer?' Cindy said, and extended her hand.

Meyer took it, smiled, and said, 'How do you do?'

She turned back to Carella almost immediately. 'Did you find what you were looking for?' she asked.

'Well, we found *something*, but I'm not sure it helps us very much.'

'Weren't the records complete?'

'Yes, fairly complete,' Carella said. 'It's just that ...'

'Did you talk to Mr Ferguson?'

'Who?'

'Ferguson. The football coach.'

'No, we didn't,' Carella said, puzzled.

'He might have been able to help you. He's been at the school for ages. The team never wins, but they keep rehiring Ferguson because he's such a nice old man.'

'I see,' Carella said.

'You might look him up.'

'Why, Cindy?'

'Well, didn't you come down to ...' She stared up into his face. 'I'm sorry, maybe I'm confused.'

'Maybe we're *all* a little confused,' Meyer said, his eyes suddenly narrowing. 'Why do you think we should have looked up the football coach, Miss Forrest?'

'Well, only because he was on the team, you see.'

'*Who* was on the team?' Carella said.

'Why, Daddy.' She paused, her blue eyes wide. 'Didn't you know he went to school here?'

*

Salvatore Palumbo was fifty-seven years old, a wiry little man who had been born in Naples, and who'd come to America in 1938 because he didn't like Mussolini or what he was doing with the country. He did not speak a word of English when he arrived, and he had only forty dollars in American money, plus a wife and two children, and the address of a cousin. He went to see the cousin in Philadelphia and the cousin made a great show of welcoming him and then promptly let it be known he wasn't really welcome at all. So Palumbo, still not speaking a word of English – this was only a week after he'd arrived – spent twenty of his American dollars for train tickets and took his family to another city, and tried to make a start.

It was not easy to make a start. In Naples, he had been a fruit vendor with a small pushcart. He used to buy his produce from the farmers who drifted into the city from the outlying districts, and he used to shove his pushcart all over the city, sometimes not getting home until nine or ten at night, but nonetheless providing a living for himself and his family. The living was poor, even by Italian standards; in Naples, Salvatore Palumbo and his wife had lived in a slum. In America, he moved from Philadelphia, where his cousin lived in a slum, directly to another city and another slum.

He did not like the slum. In Italian, he said to his wife, 'I did not come to America to live in yet another slum,' and then he set about trying to find work. He thought it might be a good idea to get himself another pushcart, but he didn't speak English at all, and he didn't know where to buy his produce, or how to go about getting a vendor's licence, or even that a vendor's licence was necessary. He got a job on the waterfront instead. He was always a small man, and lifting bales and crates was difficult for him. He developed a powerful chest and muscular arms, so that he looked like a bandy-legged little wrestler after two years of working the docks.

Well, America is the land of opportunity. That's the God's honest truth, you can take it or leave it. You don't have to stay in a slum, and you don't have to keep working on the docks. If you have the will, determination, and ambition of a man like Salvatore Palumbo, you can in twenty-five years own a little house in Riverhead – in an Italian neighbourhood, yes, but not in a slum or a ghetto – and you can have your own fruit and vegetable store seven blocks away on Dover Plains Avenue, and people will call you Sal instead of Salvatore.

At twelve noon on May 1, Detectives Meyer and Carella were

in another part of the city making a series of startling discoveries while Sal Palumbo stood on the sidewalk outside his store and polished his fruit. They discovered first of all that Anthony Forrest was a graduate of Ramsey University, a fact they had never known. And then, carried on the wave of this fresh discovery, they remembered that Mae Norden, the wife of the slain lawyer Randolph Norden, had told them her husband had studied at Ramsey Law. Like men who had found the elusive piece of a very tiring jigsaw puzzle when the piece was right there on the table all along, just under the ashtray, they exuberantly tied the first two deaths with the death of the prostitute Blanche Lettiger, who had also been a student at Ramsey, and foolishly and joyously believed the puzzle was almost finished when in actuality it had only just begun.

Sal Palumbo had no such feelings of soaring joy as he polished the fruit. He liked fruit, indeed he loved fruit, but he did not polish it because it gave him any particular pleasure. He was not the kind of person who could go wild over the colour of an apple or a pear. He polished the fruit because when it was polished it looked better to his customers, and when it looked better to his customers, they bought it. One of his customers was walking towards the store now, an Irish lady named Mrs O'Grady. He did not know the Irish lady's first name. He knew that she lived someplace in Riverhead, but not in the immediate neighbourhood. Palumbo's stand was on Dover Plains Avenue, just below the elevated structure, near the corner of 200th Street. There was a station stop on that corner, and every Tuesday afternoon at about this time, Mrs O'Grady would come down the steps leading from the station and stop first in the candy store on the corner, and then next in the butcher's shop alongside it, and then she would walk to Palumbo's store, which was two stores down from the butcher's shop in the shadow of the station platform.

'Ah, *signora*,' Palumbo said, as she approached, and she promptly answered, 'Don't give me the Eye-talian malarkey, Sal.'

Mrs O'Grady was perhaps fifty-two years old, with a trim, spare figure, and a devilish twinkle in her green eyes. She had been doing business with the merchants along Dover Plains Avenue for five years now because she liked their prices and their goods better than those available in her own neighbourhood. If you had asked either Mrs O'Grady or Sal Palumbo about the casual flirtation that had been going on between them for the past five years, both would have said you were out of your mind. Palumbo was married with two grown married sons and with three grandchildren. Mrs O'Grady was married, with a married daughter who was pregnant. But Palumbo was a man who liked women in general, not only Southern Italian types like his wife, Rose, with her dark hair and her darker eyes, but even trim little types with small compact breasts and tight small backsides and green eyes like Mrs O'Grady. And Mrs O'Grady was a passionate sort who liked nothing better than a good strong man in her arms, and this little fellow Sal Palumbo had good strong arms and a great massive chest with curling black hair showing at the open throat of his shirt. And so the two of them bandied small talk over the fruit, carrying on a flirtation that would never be openly recognized, that would never come to so much as a touch of the hand, but that nonetheless flared once a week every Tuesday over the pears and the apples and the plums and the peaches.

'Well, it don't look so good to me today, Sal,' Mrs O'Grady said. 'Is this all you've got?'

'What's the matter with you?' Palumbo demanded, his voice carrying only the faintest trace of an accent. 'Those are beautiful fruit. What do you want? You want some nice pears today? I got some apricots, too, the first of the season.'

'And bitter as poison, I'll bet.'

'From me? Bitter fruit from Sal Palumbo? Ah, *bella signora*, you know me better than that.'

'What are those melons?'

'What are they but melons? You see them with your eyes, no? You just named them. They're honeydew melons.'

'Good?'

'Beautiful.'

'How do I know?'

'Mrs O'Grady, for you I would slice one open, but only for you, and only because when I slice it open you'll find a melon so sweet, and so ripe, and so green as your own eyes.'

'Never mind my own eyes,' Mrs O'Grady said. 'And you don't

have to slice it for me, I'll take your word. No plums yet?'

'We can't rush the summer,' Palumbo answered.

'Well, let me have two pounds of the apples. How much are the apricots?'

'Thirty-nine a pound.'

'That's too high.'

'I'm losing money.'

'I'll just bet you are,' she answered, smiling.

'These have to be shipped in, you know. Refrigerator cars. The grower makes money, the shipper makes money, the railroad makes money, but by the time the apricots get to me, what do I make?'

'Well, give me a couple of pounds, so you can lose some more money.'

'Two?'

'I said a couple, didn't I?'

'*Signora*, in Italy, a couple is always two. In America, a couple can be three, four, a half a dozen. *Ma che?*' He spread his hands and shrugged his shoulders, and Mrs O'Grady laughed.

'Two pounds,' she said.

'You need some lettuce? I got nice iceberg and nice Romaine, whichever your heart desires.'

'The iceberg,' she said. 'You know who has really good fruit?'

'Sal Palumbo has really good fruit,' he answered.

'No, the fruit man in my own neighbourhood. And *his* apricots are cheaper.'

Palumbo, who was reaching over the crates stacked in front of his stand, reaching onto the slanting stand itself to the rear where his apricots were piled in neat rows, said, 'How much are his apricots?'

'Thirty-five cents a pound.'

'So then go buy *his* apricots,' Palumbo said.

'I would,' Mrs O'Grady replied, 'but he was all out of them when I got there.'

'*Signora*,' Palumbo said, 'if *I* was all out of apricots, they'd be thirty-five cents a pound, too. You want them, *si* or *no*?'

'I'll take them,' Mrs O'Grady said, her green eyes twinkling, 'but it's highway robbery.'

Palumbo opened a brown paper bag and dropped a handful of

apricots into it. He put the bag on his hanging scale and was piling more apricots into it when the bullet came from the station platform above him, entering his head at a sharp angle from the top of his skull. He fell forward onto the stand. The fruit and vegetables came tumbling down around him as he collapsed to the sidewalk, the polished pears and apples, the green peppers, the oranges and lemons and potatoes, while Mrs O'Grady looked at him in horror and then began screaming.

Chapter Eight

Carella and Meyer did not learn that an Italian fruit dealer named Salvatore Palumbo had been shot to death until they got back to the squad-room at four o'clock that afternoon of May 1. Up to that time, they had been poring over the records of Anthony Forrest and Randolph Norden at the university.

The records were puzzling and contradictory, and supplied them with almost no additional clues as to just what the hell was happening.

Anthony Forrest had entered Ramsey University as a business administration major in the spring semester of 1937, when he was eighteen years old and a graduate of Ashley High School in Majesta. By the spring of 1940, which was when Blanche Lettiger enrolled at the university, he was entering his senior year. He had been only a fair student, averaging C for almost every semester at the school, barely qualifying academically for the football team. He was graduated two hundred and fifth in his class in January of 1941, with a B.S. degree. He had been a member of the ROTC while at the college, but he was not called to active duty until almost a year after graduation, when the attack on Pearl Harbour startled the world.

Randolph Norden had entered Ramsey University in the fall of 1935, when he was eighteen years old and a graduate of Thomas Hardy High in Bethtown. He enrolled as a liberal arts major with intentions of eventually going on to Ramsey Law. In the spring of 1937, when Forrest entered the school, Norden was half-way through his sophomore year. In the spring of 1940, when Blanche Lettiger entered the school, Norden had already completed his three-year pre-law requirement and was in his second year of law school. He was graduated from Ramsey Law in June of 1941, and he went into the navy almost immediately after the attack on Pearl Harbour.

His records showed that Norden was an excellent student throughout his entire stay at Ramsey. He had been elected to the student council in his sophomore year, had made Phi Beta Kappa as a junior, was listed in *Who's Who in American Colleges and Universities*, and – in law school – was a member of The Order of the Cois, as well as editor of the *Ramsey Law Review*.

A closer search of the records showed that Randolph Norden had never been in any of Anthony Forrest's classes. Nor did it appear as though either of the men, one of whom was a graduating senior in 1940, the other of whom was in his second year of law school, had shared any classes with the entering freshman named Blanche Ruth Lettiger.

'So what do you make of it?' Carella had asked.

'I'm damned if I know,' Meyer had answered.

Now, entering the squad-room at four o'clock in the afternoon, they still did not have the answer. They stopped off in the Clerical Office and bummed two cups of coffee from Miscolo. A note on Carella's desk told him that the B.C.I. had called. It no longer seemed important to know the names of the criminals Randolph Norden had defended, but he dutifully returned the call anyway, and was talking to a man named Simmons when the other phone rang. Meyer picked it up.

'Eighty-seventh Squad, Meyer,' he said.

'Let me talk to Carella, huh?' the voice on the other end said.

'Who's this, please?'

'This is Mannheim of the one-oh-four in Riverhead.'

'Hold on a second, will you?' Meyer said. 'He's on the other line.'

'Sure,' Mannheim said.

Carella looked up.

'The one-oh-four in Riverhead,' Meyer whispered. 'Guy named Mannheim.'

Carella nodded. Into his own phone he said, 'Then all but one of them are still serving prison terms, is that right?'

'That's right,' Simmons told him.

'What's the story on the one who's loose?'

'His name's Frankie Pierce. He's been back with us since last ·

November. He was serving a five-and-dime at Castleview, came up for parole last year, was granted.'

'What was the rap?'

'Burglary three.'

'Any other arrests in his record?'

'He had a J.D. card when he was fifteen, pulled in twice on gang rumbles, but that was all.'

'Weapons?'

'A zip gun in one of the rumbles. They threw the Sullivan Act, but his lawyer got him off with a suspended sentence.'

'He was paroled in November, you say?'

'That's right.'

'Where's he living now?'

'Isola. Three-seven-one Horton. That's down here near the Calm's Point Bridge.'

'Who's his parole officer?'

'McLaughlin. You know him?'

'I think so. Any trouble?'

'He's been sound as a dollar since he got out. My guess is he'll be back at the old stand pretty soon, though. That's the pattern, ain't it?'

'Sometimes,' Carella said.

'You got some burglaries up there, is that it?' Simmons asked.

'No, this is homicide.'

'How does it look?'

'Pretty cool right now.'

'Give it time. Homicides work themselves out, don't they?'

'Not always,' Carella said. 'Thanks a lot, Simmons.'

'Don't mention it,' he said, and hung up. Carella pressed the extension button.

'Hello?' he said.

'Carella?'

'Yep.'

'This is Mannheim, the one-oh-four in Riverhead.'

'How are you, Mannheim?'

'Fine, fine. Listen, you the guy who's handling this sniper case?'

'I'm the guy. Have you got something for me?'

'Yeah,' Mannheim said.

'What is it?'
'Another stiff.'

*

Rose Palumbo spoke very bad English even when she was coherent, and she was practically incoherent by the time Carella reached her at the old frame house in Riverhead. They tried sparring in the King's language for a while, with her repeating something about 'atops' that Carella didn't understand at all until one of her sons, a man named Richard Palumbo, told Carella she was worried about them cutting up her husband when they did an autopsy. Carella tried to assure the woman, in English, that all they were interested in establishing was the cause of, death, but the woman kept repeating the word 'atops' between her flowing tears and her violent gasps for breath until Carella finally took her shoulders and shook her.

'*Ma che vergogna, signora!*' he shouted.

'*Mi dispiace,*' Rose said, '*ma non posso sopportare l'idea che lo taglino. Perchè devono tagliare?*'

'*Perchè l'hanno ucciso,*' Carella said, '*e vogliamo scoprire chi è stato.*'

'*Ma che scoprirete tagliandolo?*'

'*La palla è ancora dentro. Dobbiamo trovare la palla perchè ci sono stati altri morti. Altri tre.*'

'*E tagliarono gli altri?*'

'*Si.*'

'*È peccato contro Dio mutilare i morti.*'

'*È un più grosso peccato contro Dio di uccidere,*' Carella answered.

'What's she saying?' Meyer asked.

'She doesn't want an autopsy.'

'Tell her we don't need her permission.'

'How's that going to help? She's out of her mind with grief.' He turned back to the woman. '*Signora,*' he said, '*è necessario individuare il tipo di pallottola che l'ho uccise. La palla è ancora dentro, non comprende? Dobbiamo sapere che tipo.*'

'*Si, si, capisco.*'

'*È per questo che dobbiamo fare un'autopsia. Comprende? Così potremo trovare l'assassino.*'

'*Si, si, capisco.*'

'*La prego, signora. Provi.*' He patted her on the shoulder, and then turned to the son, Richard. Richard was perhaps thirty years old, a strapping man with broad shoulders and a dancer's narrow waist. 'We'd like to ask you a few questions, Mr Palumbo, is that all right?'

'You have to excuse my mother,' Palumbo said. 'She doesn't speak English too well.'

'That's all right,' Carella said.

'My father spoke pretty good English, though not when he first came here. He really worked at it. But my mother ...' Richard shook his head. 'I guess she always felt America was a temporary thing, a stop along the way. I think she always planned to go back to Naples, you know? But not my father. This was it. For him, this was it. He'd really found the place. So he learned the language. He really learned it pretty good. A little accent, but not too noticeable. He was quite a guy.'

Richard said all this looking at a point somewhere above Carella's shoulders, not looking into Carella's eyes or even his face. He delivered the words as though he were saying a prayer over Palumbo's open grave. There were no tears in his eyes, but his face was white, and he kept focusing on that imaginary point somewhere above Carella's shoulder, staring.

'He worked hard all his life,' Richard said. 'When we first came to this country, I was just a little kid. That was in nineteen thirty-eight, that was a long time ago. I was eight years old. My brother was only three. We didn't have nothing to eat then, you know? My father worked like a horse on the docks. He was a skinny little guy then, you shoulda seen him. Then he got all these muscles from lifting all that heavy stuff, you know? He was quite a guy, my father.' He gestured towards the small, framed picture of Palumbo where it stood on the living-room mantelpiece. 'He made all this himself, you know – the house, the store. From nothing. Saved up his pennies, learned English, got himself a pushcart at first with the money he saved from the docks. Just like when he was in Naples, he used to push that damn pushcart all over the city, he used to be exhausted when he got home at night. I remember he used to yell at me, and once he even slapped me, not because he was sore at me, but only because he was so .

damn tired. But he made it, huh? He got his own store, didn't he? He had a good business, my father. He was a real good man.'

Carella looked at Meyer, and neither said a word.

'So somebody kills him' Richard said. 'Somebody shoots him from up there on the train station.' He paused. 'What did he do to anybody? He never hurt anybody in his entire life. Only once did he ever slap even me, his own son, and that was because he was so tired, not because he was sore, he never hit anybody in anger, he never hit anybody at all. So he's dead.'

Richard gave a slight shrug, and his hands moved in a futile, bewildered gesture.

'How do you figure it? I don't know. How do you make any sense out of it? He worked all his damn life to have his store, to take care of his family, and then somebody just shoots him, like as if he was ... *nothing*. That's my *father* that guy shot, don't he know that? That's my father they took away in the ambulance. For Christ's sake, don't he realize that, the guy who shot him? Don't he realize this is my father who's dead now?'

Tears were welling into his eyes. He kept staring at the spot above Carella's shoulder.

'Ain't *he* got a father, that guy? How could he just ... just *shoot* him like that, how could he make himself pull the trigger? This is a man who was standing down there, a man, my *father*, for Christ's sake! Don't he know what he done? Don't he know this man is never gonna go to his store again, he's never gonna argue with the customers, he's never gonna laugh or nothing? How could he do that, will you tell me?'

Richard paused. His voice lowered. 'I didn't even see him today. He left the house before I got up this morning. My wife and I, we live right upstairs. Every morning I usually meet him, we leave about the same time to go to work. I work in an aircraft-parts factory on Two Thirty-third. But this morning, I had a little virus, I was running a small fever, my wife said stay in bed, so she called in sick. And I didn't get to see my father. Not even to say, "Hello, Pop, how's it going?" So today, somebody kills him. The day I didn't see him.'

'Have you got any idea who might have done this?' Carella asked.

'No.'

'Has anyone been threatening your father? Had he received any notes or phone calls, or . . .'

'No.'

'Any trouble with any of the businessmen along the avenue?'

'None.' Richard shook his head again. 'Everybody liked him. This don't make sense. Everybody liked him.' He rubbed at his nose with his forefinger, sniffed, and said again, 'I didn't even see him today. Not even to say hello.'

Chapter Nine

The next morning, Wednesday, May 2, Steve Carella went in to see Detective Lieutenant Byrnes. He told the lieutenant that the case was taking some unexpected twists, that he and Meyer thought they'd had at least something to go on, but that they weren't quite so sure of that any more, and that there was a strong possibility the killer was a nut. In view of the circumstances, Carella told the lieutenant, he would like additional help from whomever Byrnes could spare on the squad, and he would also like to request that Byrnes put in for help from the other squads in the city, since the killer seemed to be moving from place to place, and since legwork alone was taking up a considerable amount of time that could just possibly go into deduction, if there was anything to deduce, which there didn't seem to be at the moment.

Byrnes listened to everything Carella had to say, and told him he would do everything he could as soon as he had a chance to look over his duty schedules and to call the Chief of Detectives downtown at headquarters. But Carella had to wait until much later that day before he got the help he requested. And then, unexpectedly, the help came from the district attorney's office.

Andrew Mulligan was an assistant district attorney who wanted to be governor of the state one day, and after that – now that Kennedy had broken the ground for Catholics – he figured it might be nice to be president. His office was downtown on High Street adjacent to the Criminal Courts Building, just across the street from police headquarters. Byrnes had placed his call to the Chief of Detectives at precisely 11.15 a.m., but Mulligan didn't know that, since he'd been in court at the time. In fact, Mulligan had no notion that the men of the 87th Squad were working on four possibly related murders, nor did he have any idea that he would soon be helping them with the case. At the moment, he was working with the D.A. himself on a case involving income tax evasion. Mulligan didn't know that the D.A. himself wanted to be governor of the state, too, but even if he had known, it wouldn't have bothered him. The particular case they were trying together involved a very big-shot racketeer and was getting a lot of headlines in the local press. Mulligan liked headlines. It annoyed him that there was a jazz musician named Gerry Mulligan, who wasn't even a relation. He felt that when anyone mentioned the name Mulligan, or whenever the name Mulligan appeared in print, it should instantly bring to mind the image of a fighting assistant district attorney, and not some crummy bongo drummer, or whatever this other Mulligan was.

He had, in fairness to the case he would soon become a part of, tried four murder cases since he'd begun working with the D.A.'s office. He liked murder cases because they usually guaranteed a lot of newspaper coverage. His first murder case had been brought to him by the detectives of the 49th Squad, an open and shut Murder One that anyone fresh out of law school could have tried successfully. Mulligan milked the case for all it was worth. The trial should have been over and done with in two weeks at the most. Mulligan stretched it to a month, with headlines screaming every day, and would have stretched it even further if the judge hadn't begun issuing some subtle hints about the 'seemingly inexhaustible supply of rhetoric at this trial'. Mulligan got his headlines, and he also got his conviction, and then – because nothing succeeds like success, that's how the saying goes, go tell it to Larry Parks – he was assigned another murder case shortly thereafter, and then another, and then yet another, the number of murders committed in that fair city being almost as inexhaustible as the supply of rhetoric at his first trial.

As he left the court-house and walked down the broad flat steps in front of the building, he was wondering what he'd be working on after they had demolished this cheap racketeer with his phony meat market covering up a multi-million-dollar vice ring. He did not know he would become involved in the case the 87th was now working on, but he certainly hoped his next one would be another murder trial. He was also thinking about what he would order for lunch.

The restaurant he habitually frequented was off on one of the side streets bordering the financial district. Most of the lawyers who had any traffic with the downtown courts lunched there, and he enjoyed the quiet buzz that usually accompanied his entrance into the place. He had no idea what any of the attorneys were whispering about him behind their hands, but he was sure it was good. As he entered the restaurant that afternoon, he saw two young lawyers interrupt their conversation and turn in his direction. He did not acknowledge their stares in any way. He stood unobtrusively immense just inside the doorway, the court-room dynamo in his civilian disguise, and waited for the proprietress of the restaurant to discover him.

She discovered him almost immediately.

'Oh, Mr Mulligan,' she said, distressed. 'I did not know you were coming today. Your table is taken.'

'Oh?' Mulligan said, his eyebrows raising just a trifle, an only faintly interested expression on his face. 'Didn't my secretary call?'

'No, Mr Mulligan, I'm sorry. She didn't.'

'Well . . .' Mulligan said, and he turned a gently anticipatory inquiring look on the flustered proprietress, a look that firmly demanded, 'Well, what do you propose to do about this intolerable set of circumstances?'

The proprietress knew how to read looks because she'd been dealing with lawyers both here and in the old country, and they were all the same, they all stank.

'I'll get you another table, Mr Mulligan,' she said, 'a very nice table in the other room. Come with me, I'll take care of you.'

She started to turn, and then stopped in her tracks, and a smile flowered on her face, and she said, 'Wait, they're leaving. Look, they're just paying their check. See, Mr Mulligan? It all turned out all right, after all. You can have your own table.'

'I appreciate that,' Mulligan said. 'Sincerely, I do.'

The two gentlemen sitting at Mulligan's customary table paid the check, rose, lighted their cigars, and left the restaurant. The waiter changed the tablecloth, and held the chair for Mulligan as he sat. Mulligan pulled the chair close to the table and, without looking at the waiter, said, 'Dewar's on the rocks, please,' and then relaxed and looked through the huge plate-glass window at the street outside. He enjoyed sitting in the same spot each day

83

because it made him easier to identify. He particularly enjoyed this table immediately adjacent to the window because it enabled him to be identified from *outside* the restaurant as well as inside. A fellow attorney passed the table, said, 'Hello, Andy, how are you?' and touched him on the shoulder. Mulligan smiled in response and wondered where the hell his Scotch was. The waiter brought it almost instantly.

'Would you like to order now, Mr Mulligan?' the waiter asked.

'I'll look over the menu,' Mulligan said. The waiter brought the card, and Mulligan picked up his glass of Scotch, took a sip of it, and began reading. The menu rarely changed. He almost knew it by heart.

He was wondering whether he should have the crabmeat au gratin when suddenly the plate-glass window alongside the table shattered.

Mulligan didn't have time to react to the falling glass because it had been shattered by a bullet, and the next thing the bullet shattered was the bone just below his right temple.

*

If there had been a scale of importance for homicide, ranging from zero for the least important to ten for the most important, Blanche Lettiger would have clocked in at zero, Sal Palumbo would have registered a resounding two, and both Anthony Forrest and Randolph Norden would have fallen somewhere between the three and four mark.

Andrew Mulligan fell snoot first into his glass of Dewar's on the rocks and promptly sent the murder meter soaring to seven point eight. There were two leading afternoon newspapers in the city, one big, one small, you paid your money and you took your choice. They both stank. The big one always printed its headline-above-the-headline in red type. The tabloid-sized one always printed its headline-above-the-headline in blue type, because it was a very liberal newspaper and didn't want people to think it was *too* liberal, in fact didn't want even the slightest association with the colour red. The big newspaper's headline that afternoon read SNIPER SLAYS D.A. The headline-above-the-headline was printed in red and it said: MULLIGAN'S TRIUMPHS, p. 5. The tabloid-sized newspaper's headline that afternoon read MUL-

LIGAN MURDERED, and across the top of the page, in blue, THE FIGHTING D.A., A Study by Agnes Lovely, p. 33. Agnes Lovely's study had been composed in fifteen minutes by back-tracking through the paper's morgue shortly before press time. The *news* story, on the other hand, read more like a study because it was a policy of the blue-headline tabloid to make every item of news sound like a piece of fiction in a popular magazine. If President Kennedy sent a new tax bill to Congress, the blue-headline tabloid started the story something like this: *These ancient halls were still with contemplation today. There was a paper to be considered, a decision to be made. The paper had come down to them from above, a document that could change the lives of everyone in the nation, a document that . . .* and so on. Somewhere towards the end of the news story, the reporter usually revealed what the hell he was talking about. Up to that time, he was writing for atmosphere and suspense.

There were many people in the city who felt that the rifle death of an assistant district attorney contained enough atmosphere and suspense all by itself. These people foolishly felt that all a newspaper was supposed to do in a news story was tell the facts, ma'am. But the blue-headline newspaper, you see, was really running a disguised school for fiction writers, someone having told the city editor that Ernest Hemingway had once been a newspaper correspondent. The city editor also felt that most of the people in the city were illiterate. He would have liked to fill his newspaper with a lot of photographs beneath which would be short sharp captions, but a morning newspaper in the city had been using that format for a good many years now, and the city editor of the blue-headline tabloid didn't want to seem like a copycat. So instead, he decided that illiterate people would rather not have their news straight from the shoulder, but would instead prefer reading each story as if it were a chapter of a long novel about life.

The tall man was drinking Scotch.
He sat by the restaurant window
watching the rush of humanity outside, thinking private thoughts of
a crusader who has foolishly and
momentarily taken off all his arm-

or. He could have been a Columbus in
other times, he could have been an Es-
sex at the side of Elizabeth. He was,
instead, a tall and impressive man
drinking his Scotch. He was soon to
be a dead man.

This was the way the reporter on the blue-headline newspaper started his story. But in addition to a city editor who had the notion that everyone was an illiterate except maybe himself, the paper also had a typesetter who thought that people enjoyed working out cryptograms while reading their newspapers. When you were dealing with illiterates, it wasn't necessary to give the facts in the first place, and in the second place it was always necessary to garble every line of type so that the story became even more mystifying and, in many cases, practically unintelligible.

The story on page 3 of that afternoon's edition read like this:

Thet allman was drinking Scotch.
He sat by the restaurant window
watching the Russian humanity outside, thinking private thoughts of
sex at the side of Elizabeth. He was,
a crusader who has foolishly and
momentarily taken off all his arm.
Or he could have been a Columbus in
other times, he could have been an Es
DRINKING HIS SCOTCH. He was
soon to be a dead man.
instead, a tall and impressive man.

It really didn't matter what the blue-headline tabloid said, because the assistant district attorney named Andrew Mulligan was inconsiderately turning a little blue on a slab in the morgue, and the District Attorney himself, a man named Carter Cole, turned a very deep shade of blue mixed with red and bordering on purple when he found out that a man from his office had been inconveniently knocked off in the middle of a trial while drinking a glass of Scotch.

The D.A. himself picked up a telephone and put in a call to the Police Commissioner, wanting to know what the hell was happening in this city when a respected and much-needed assistant district attorney couldn't even go to a restaurant without having his brains blown out while drinking a glass of Scotch. The Police Commissioner told him that he was doing everything in his power to get at the facts, after which he hung up and called the Chief of Detectives.

He asked the Chief of Detectives what the hell was happening in this city when a respected and much-needed assistant district attorney couldn't even go into a restaurant without having his brains blown out while drinking a glass of Scotch. The Chief of Detectives told him that he was doing everything in his power to get at the facts, after which he hung up and called Detective Lieutenant Peter Byrnes of the 87th Squad.

Detective Lieutenant Peter Byrnes informed the Chief of Detectives that he had called him only this morning in an attempt to solicit some assistance on this case which was getting a little out of hand, what with people dying like flies, and what with respected and much-needed assistant district attorneys getting their brains blown out and all. The Chief of Detectives told Lieutenant Byrnes that he would certainly see to it that Capello, or whatever his name was, got all the help he needed on this case because, and here his voice lowered, and he actually said, 'Just between you and me, Pete,' the D.A. himself was a little burned up over the situation.

Andrew Mulligan, meanwhile, was being sliced up nicely and neatly, and being searched for a stray bullet which, when it was found, turned out to be a Remington .308, of all things. Being dead, he still had no idea that Carella and Meyer of the 87th Squad were working on a case involving someone who was putting bullets through people's heads, nor had he any idea how much his own death had helped the investigating cops.

By midnight that night, Carella had been assigned teams of detectives from every section of the city to assist in running down the sniper. He had, in effect, a small army to work with.

Now, all the army had to do was find the enemy.

Chapter Ten

The enemy, like all good enemies everywhere, vanished from sight.

There were no subsequent killings that week, and it seemed indeed as though detectives from all over the city had been mobilized to combat a ghost. Thursday, Friday, and Saturday passed uneventfully. The cruellest month was gone, taking part of May with it, and the murderer seemed to have disappeared.

On Sunday, May 6, two detectives from the 12th Precinct, near the Calm's Point Bridge downtown, decided it would be a good idea to look up Frankie Pierce. Carella had mentioned the name casually to them, as that of an ex-con who had once been a client of Randolph Norden. He had also mentioned that, in view of later developments, it seemed to him Pierce was clean, and not worth picking up. But the two detectives from the 12th were Detectives/1st Grade, and Carella was only a Detective/2nd Grade, and they didn't much like being told how to investigate a homicide by someone whom they outranked, even if the squeal happened to be Carella's. Besides, the two detectives from the 12th were bulls.

One was named Masterson, and the other was named Brock. The two had been working together as a pair for a long time, and they had a long series of arrests and convictions to their credit, but they were nonetheless bulls. On that first Sunday in May, with the carnelian cherry blossoms bursting in the park, and a mild breeze blowing in off the River Dix from the South, Masterson and Brock got a little restless in the stuffy squad-room of the 12th, and decided they could use a little fresh air. And then, since they were simply cruising around the streets in the vicinity of the Calm's Point Bridge, they decided to look up Frankie Pierce who lived at 371 Horton in the bridge's shadow.

Frankie Pierce had no idea he was about to be visited by

detectives, or by detectives who were bulls. He was in constant touch with his parole officer, and he knew he had done nothing to break parole. He was, in fact, working at a garage as a mechanic and he had every intention of going straight like they say in the movies. His employer was a fair-minded man who knew Frankie was on parole, but who felt that a man deserves a chance at rehabilitation. Frankie was a good worker and a hard worker. His employer was satisfied with him and had given him a raise only the month before.

But Frankie made a couple of mistakes on that first Sunday in May when the bulls named Masterson and Brock visited him. The first mistake he made was in assuming the two detectives were only detectives and not bulls. The second mistake he made was in believing that people are understanding.

He had a date that afternoon with a girl who was the cashier in a restaurant near the garage. He had told the girl he was an ex-con because he wanted to get things straight with her from the start. The girl had looked him over very carefully and then said, 'What do I care what you used to be?' and that was that. He was going to take her over to the park, where they would go rowing for a while, and then have dinner at the outdoor restaurant, and then maybe walk up the Stem and take in a movie later. He was standing before the mirror putting on his tie when the knock sounded on his door.

'Who is it?' he asked.

'Police. Open up, Frankie.'

A puzzled look crossed his face. He looked at himself in the mirror, as though expecting an answer from his own image, then shrugged and walked to the door.

Masterson and Brock stood in the hallway. They were both well over six feet tall, each weighing about two hundred pounds, both wearing slacks and short-sleeved sports shirts that showed the bulge of their chest and arm muscles. Frankie, standing in front of them in the open door, looked very small, even though he was five feet ten inches tall and weighed a hundred and sixty-five pounds.

'Frankie Pierce?' Masterson asked.

'That's right,' he answered.

'Get your hat, Frankie,' Masterson said.

'What's the matter?'

'We want to talk to you.'

'What about?'

'Get your hat.'

'I don't wear a hat. What's the matter?'

'We want to ask you a few questions, Frankie.'

'Well . . . well, why don't you ask them then?'

'You gonna be a wise guy?' Brock asked suddenly. It was the first time he had spoken, and the effect of his words was chilling. He had slate-grey eyes and a thick nose, and a mouth drawn across his face with a draughtsman's pen, tight and hard, and barely moving when he spoke.

'No, look,' Frankie said. 'I don't mind answering some questions. It's just I have a date, that's all.'

'You want to finish tying your tie, Frankie?' Masterson asked. 'Or do you want to come along the way you are?'

'Well . . . well, I'd like to tie my tie and . . . you know, I want to polish my shoes and . . .' He hesitated. 'I told you, I have a date.'

'Yeah, you told us. Go tie your tie.'

'Is this gonna take long?'

'That depends on you, don't it, Frankie?'

'What do you mean?'

'Tie your tie.'

He went to the mirror and finished the Windsor knot he had started. He was annoyed when he noticed his hands were trembling. He looked in the mirror at the two detectives who waited for him just inside the door, wondering if they had noticed, too, that his hands were trembling.

'You want to shake a leg, Frankie?' Masterson said.

'Sure, be right with you,' Frankie said pleasantly. 'I wish you guys would tell me what this is all about.'

'You'll find out, Frankie.'

'I mean, if you think I broke parole or something, you can give my parole officer a call, his name's McLaughlin, he can tell you . . .'

'We don't have to give nobody a call,' Brock said in that same chilling voice.

'Well . . . well, okay, let me just put on my jacket.'

He put on his jacket, and then walked to the door, and followed the detectives out, and locked the door behind him. There were a lot of people on the front stoop of the building and hanging around the candy store, and he was embarrassed because he knew everybody in the neighbourhood could smell a cop from away the hell across the street, and he didn't want anybody to think he was in trouble again. He kept telling himself all the way crosstown to the station house that he wasn't in trouble, this was probably some kind of routine pick-up, somebody done something, so they were naturally rounding up all the ex-cons in the neighbourhood, something like that. It would just be a matter of explaining to them, of making them understand he was going straight, had a good job with a good salary, wasn't even seeing any of the guys he used to run with before he got busted.

The two detectives said hello to the desk sergeant on their way into the building, and then Brock said in his chilling voice, 'No calls, Mike,' and they walked him to the back of the building where the detective squad-room was, and then into the squad-room itself, and then into a small room with the word INTERROGATION lettered on the frosted glass door. Brock closed the door, took a key out of his pocket, locked the door, and put the key in his pocket.

'Sit down, Frankie,' Masterson said.

Frankie sat. He had heard what Brock said to the desk sergeant, and he had seen Brock lock the door and put the key in his pocket, and he was beginning to think that maybe something very serious had been done, and he wanted no part of it, whatever the hell it was. At the same time, he knew he was an ex-con, and he knew that it was only natural for them to go looking up a guy with a record if something was done, but once he explained, once they understood he was straight now . . .

'How long you been out, Frankie?' Masterson asked.

'Since November fifteenth.'

'Castleview?'

'Yeah.'

'What were you in for?'

'Third-degree burglary.'

'You were a good boy, huh?'

'Well, yeah, I didn't give nobody any trouble.'

'That's nice, Frankie,' Masterson said.

'How long you been living down there on Horton?' Brock asked.

'Since I got out.'

'You working?'

'Yeah. I got a job.'

'Where?'

'The Esso station near the bridge. Right where the approach ...'

'What do you do there?'

'I'm a mechanic.'

'Yeah?'

'Yeah, I worked in the automobile shop up at Castle –'

'Doing what? Making licence plates?' Masterson said, and Brock laughed. His laugh was a curious thing. It never made a sound. It came into his throat and erupted there only as a series of muscular spasms.

'No, I learned a trade,' Frankie said. 'Listen, I was good enough for the garage to hire me.'

'That's nice, Frankie,' Masterson said.

'What's this all about?' Frankie asked. 'Somebody pull a job?'

'Yeah, somebody pulled a job.'

'Well, it wasn't me,' Frankie said. 'I learned my lesson.'

'Did you?'

'Five years was enough for me.' He shook his head. 'No more. Never again.'

'It's good to hear that, Frankie,' Masterson said.

'Well, I happen to mean it. I'm making eighty bucks a week now, and I work like a dog for it, but it's clean, you know. They deduct all the taxes from it, and what's left is mine, earned honest, no problems. I report once a week to my parole ...'

'Yeah, Frankie, you know a guy named Randolph Norden?'

'Sure I do. He was my lawyer.'

'*Was?*'

'Yeah. When I had the trouble. Was. Why? What's the matter?'

'How do you feel about him, Frankie?'

'He's a good lawyer. Why?'

'A good lawyer? He got you sent up, didn't he?'

'That wasn't his fault. He wanted me to plead not guilty, but this guy I knew, he was a kid in and out of jail since he could walk, he told me I should cop out, that maybe I'd get a suspended sentence. So I argued with Norden, and he kept saying not guilty, not guilty, but I told him I'd decided to cop out. So I copped out, and got ten years. Some jerk I was, huh?'

'So you liked Norden, huh?'

'Yeah, he was okay.'

'Maybe he shoulda argued a little more, don't you think? Convinced you? Don't you think that's what a good lawyer shoulda done?'

'He tried to, but I wouldn't listen. I figured all I had on my record so far was juvenile stuff, you know, rumbles, and once when I was carrying a zip gun, the Sullivan Act. But I figured, what it amounted to, the burglary rap was a first offence really, and I figured if I copped out they'd go easy, maybe make it a suspended sentence. Instead, we got a judge he figured I'd learn a lesson behind bars for a little while.' Frankie shrugged. 'Maybe he was right.'

'You're a pretty nice fellow, ain't you, Frankie? You forgive Norden for steering you wrong, and now you're forgiving the judge for sending you away. That's real nice of you, Frankie.'

'A judge only has a job to do,' Frankie said, and he shrugged again. 'Listen, I don't understand what this is all about. What's this got to do with . . .'

'With *what*, Frankie?'

'With . . . well, with *whatever*. With . . . with why you dragged me up here. What's the story?'

'You read the papers, Frankie?'

'Sometimes.'

'When's the last time?'

'I don't know. I go to work early, and I ain't got time to stop for them. Anyway, I don't read so good. That's why I got in all that trouble when I was still in high school. Everybody else was reading . . .'

'Yeah, let's never mind the underprivileged kid bit, Frankie,' Masterson said. 'When's the last time you read a newspaper?'

'I don't know. I just told you . . .'

'You listen to the radio?' Brock asked in his even, emotionless voice.

'Sure I do.'

'You heard about the guy who's going around shooting people?'

'What guy?'

'The sniper.'

'Yeah, I think I heard something about it. Yeah, that's right, he shot some guy up in Riverhead, didn't he? A fruit man or something. Yeah, I heard that.' Frankie looked up at the detectives, puzzled. 'I don't get it. What ... what ...?'

'All right, let's cut the crap,' Brock said, and the room went silent.

Frankie looked up at them expectantly, and they looked down at him patiently, waiting. Frankie wasn't sure what crap he was expected to cut, but he suddenly wanted that door to be unlocked, suddenly wanted that telephone to ring. The two detectives stood over him silently, and he looked up at them silently, each waiting, he not knowing what he was expected to say or do, they seemingly possessed of infinite patience. He wiped his upper lip. He shrugged, The silence lengthened unbearably. He could hear the clock ticking on the wall.

'Look,' he said at last, 'could you tell me what ...?' and Brock hit him. He hit him suddenly and effortlessly, his arm coming up swiftly from its position at his side, his hand open, his palm catching Frankie noisily on the cheek. Frankie was more surprised than hurt. He brought his hands up too late, felt the stinging slap, and then looked up at Brock with a puzzled expression.

'What'd I do?' he asked plaintively.

'Randolph Norden is dead, Frankie,' Masterson said.

Frankie sat still for several moments, looking up at the detectives, sweating freely now, feeling trapped in this small room with its locked door. 'What ... what do you want from me?'

Brock hit him again. He hit him very hard this time, drawing back his fist and smashing it full into Frankie's face. Frankie felt the hard knuckles colliding with his nose, and he said, 'What are you doing?' and started to come out of the chair, when Masterson put both meaty hands on his shoulders and slammed him down again, so hard that the shock rumbled up his spine and into his neck. 'Hey!' he said, and Brock hit him once more, and this time Frankie felt something break in his nose, heard the terrible crunching sound of his own nose breaking, and then immediately touched his upper lip and felt the blood pouring onto his hand.

'Why'd you do it, Frankie?' Brock said tightly.

'I didn't do nothing. Listen, will you listen . . .'

Brock bunched his fist and raised it over his head as if he were holding a hammer in it, and then brought it down as if the fist itself were the head of the hammer, onto the bridge of Frankie's nose, and Frankie screamed in pain and fell out of the chair. Masterson kicked him in the ribs, once, sharply.

'Get up,' Brock said.

'Look, look, will you please . . .?'

'*Get up!*'

He struggled to his feet. There was an unbearable pain in his nose, and blood was dripping onto his lip and all over his white shirt and the new tie he had bought for his afternoon date.

'Listen,' he said, 'listen to me. I've got a job, I'm working, I'm straight, can't you understand . . .?' and Brock hit him. 'Listen!' he screamed. '*Listen to me!* I didn't do anything! You hear me? Can you understand me?' and Brock hit him again because Brock did not understand him at all. Brock understood only that Frankie Pierce was a punk who had been cutting up other punks in street rumbles since the time he was twelve. He understood only that the punk named Frankie Pierce had graduated into the cheap thief who was Frankie Pierce, and then into the jailbird, and then into the ex-con, all of which still made him a punk, that was the understanding Brock had. So he kept following him around the room while Frankie backed against the walls trying to explain that he was straight now, he was honest, he was working, kept hitting the broken nose over and over again until it was only a sodden shapeless mass plastered to his face, don't you understand, hit him as Frankie reached for the phone and tried to pick up the receiver, won't you please understand, kicked him when he fell to the floor whimpering in pain, please, please, understand, and then stood over him with his fists bunched and ready and yelled, 'Why'd you kill him, you little son of a bitch?' and hit him again when he couldn't answer.

The girl waited for Frankie in the park for two hours. He never showed up for the date because Brock and Masterson kept him in the locked interrogation room for six hours, alternately rousing him and then beating him senseless again, while asking why he had killed a man he hadn't seen in five years. At the end of their session, they were convinced he was clean. They wrote out a report stating he had broken parole by assaulting a police officer during a routine interrogation.

Frankie Pierce was removed to the criminal ward of the hospital on Walker Island in the River Dix, to recuperate before he was shipped back to the penitentiary at Castleview, upstate.

Chapter Eleven

A sure sign that nothing was happening on this case – oh, yeah, maybe a cheap hood was being beaten up and made to realize you can't go home again – was the fact that time was passing. It was true that there had been no murders since Andrew Mulligan drank his last drink, but time was nonetheless flitting by, and there was no greater proof of this than the reappearance of Bert Kling at the squad-room, looking tanned and healthy and very blond from the sun after his vacation. Lieutenant Byrnes, who didn't like to see anyone looking so well-rested, immediately assigned him to the Sniper Case.

On the afternoon of May 7, while Meyer and Carella were uptown re-questioning Mrs O'Grady, the nice little woman who had been present when Salvatore Palumbo called it quits, Bert Kling was in the office looking over the Sniper file and trying to acquaint himself with what had gone before. When the blonde young lady walked into the squad-room, he barely looked up.

Meyer and Carella were sitting in the living-room of a two-story clapboard dwelling in Riverhead while Mrs O'Grady poured them coffee and tried to recall the incidents preceding the death of Salvatore Palumbo.

'I think he was weighing out some fruit. Do you take cream and sugar?'

'Black for me,' Meyer said.

'Detective Carella?'

'A little of each.'

'Should I call you Detective Carella, or Mr Carella, or just what?'

'Whichever is most comfortable to you.'

'Well, if you don't mind, I'll call you Mr Carella. Because calling you Detective Carella sounds as if you should be calling me Housewife O'Grady. Is that all right?'

'That's fine, Mrs O'Grady. He was weighing out some fruit, you said.'

'Yes.'

'And then what? I know we've been over all this, but . . .'

'Then he just fell onto the stand and slid down to the sidewalk. I guess I began screaming.'

'Did you hear the shot, Mrs O'Grady?'

'Yes.'

'When?'

'Just before the train pulled in.'

'What train?'

'The train. Upstairs.'

'The elevated?'

'Yes.'

'It was coming into the platform when Mr Palumbo got shot?'

'Well, to tell you the truth,' Mrs O'Grady said, 'I'm not too clear about the sequence. I mean, I heard the shot, but at the time I didn't think it was a shot, I figured it was a backfire or a blowout, who expects to hear a gun go off while you're buying fruit from a man? So, although I heard the shot, I didn't realize Sal . . . Mr Palumbo . . . had been shot. I thought he was suffering a heart attack or something, him falling like that, and the fruit all tumbling off the stand. But then, of course, I saw the blood at the back of his head, and I guess my mind made the connexion between the explosion I had heard and the fact that Sal was . . . well, I didn't know he was dead . . . but certainly hurt.'

'And the train?'

'Well, what I'm trying to say is that everything happened so fast. The train coming in . . . I think it was coming in, though it may have been leaving . . . and the shot, and Sal falling down hurt. It all happened so fast that I'm not sure of the time sequence, the poor man.'

'You're not sure, then, whether the train was pulling into the station or leaving it.'

'That's right. But it was moving, that's for sure. It wasn't just standing still in the station.'

'Did you see anyone on the station platform, Mrs O'Grady?'

'No, I didn't even look up there. I thought it was a backfire at first, you see, or something like that. It never crossed my mind that somebody was shooting a gun. So I had no reason to look around to see who or what it was. Besides, I was buying fruit, and to tell you the truth, the shot didn't register on my mind at all, either as a backfire or *anything*, it just didn't register until I began thinking about it afterwards, *after* Sal was dead, do you know what I mean? It's hard to explain, but there are so *many* noises in the city, and you just don't listen to them any more, you just go about your business.'

'Then, in effect, you really *didn't* hear the shot at the time. Or at least, you didn't react to it.'

'That's right. But there was a shot.' Mrs O'Grady paused. 'Why are you asking? Do they make silencers for rifles?'

'They're not manufactured, Mrs O'Grady, no. There are both state and federal regulations against the use of silencers. But any fairly competent machinist could turn one out in his own garage, especially if he had something like murder on his mind.'

'I always thought silencers were very complicated things. They always look so complicated in the movies.'

'Well, they're really very simple in principle. When you put a silencer on a gun or a rifle, you're closing a series of doors, in effect. You're muffling the sound.'

'Doors?' Mrs O'Grady asked.

'Try to visualize a piece of tubing, Mrs O'Grady, perhaps an inch and a half in diameter, and about eight inches long. Inside this tube is a series of separated eight-inch baffling plates, the closed "doors" that absorb the sound. That's a silencer. A man can fashion one on a home lathe.'

'Well, I heard a shot,' Mrs O'Grady said.

'And yet you didn't turn, you didn't look up, you didn't comment upon it to Mr Palumbo.'

'No.'

'The rifle that fired a three-oh-eight-calibre bullet would have been a high-powered rifle, Mrs O'Grady. Powerful enough to have felled a charging lion.'

'So?'

'It would have made a pretty loud noise.'

'So?'

'I'm only suggesting, Mrs O'Grady, that your reconstruction

of what happened may only be a result of your later thoughts about the incident.'

'I heard a shot,' Mrs O'Grady insisted.

'Did you? Or is it only now, now that you know Mr Palumbo was shot and killed, that you think you remember hearing a shot? In other words, Mrs O'Grady, is logic interfering with your memory?'

'Logic?'

'Yes. If a bullet was fired, and if a man was killed, there must have been a shot. And if there was a shot, you must have heard it. And if you heard it, you must have dismissed it as a backfire or a blowout.'

'I'm sure that's what happened.'

'Have you ever heard a blowout, Mrs O'Grady?'

'Yes, I think so.'

'And what happened? Did you ignore it, or were you momentarily startled?'

'I suppose I was startled.'

'Yet when Mr Palumbo was killed with a high-powered rifle which would have made a very loud noise, you only *later* remembered hearing a shot. Does that sound valid?'

'Well, I *think* I heard a shot,' Mrs O'Grady said.

Carella smiled. 'Maybe you did,' he answered. 'We'll check with the man in the change booth on the platform. In any case, Mrs O'Grady, you've been extremely co-operative and most helpful.'

'He was a nice man,' Mrs O'Grady said. 'Sal. He was really a very nice man.'

*

The man in the change booth at the station platform above Palumbo's store was not a very nice man at all. He was a crotchety old grouch who began giving the detectives trouble the moment they approached the booth.

'How many?' he asked immediately.

'How many what?' Meyer asked.

'Can't you read the sign? State how many tokens you want.'

'We don't want any tokens,' Meyer said.

'Map of the system is on the wall right there,' the attendant said. 'I'm not paid to give out travel information.'

'Are you paid to co-operate with the police?' Carella asked amiably.

'The what?'

'Police,' Meyer said, and he flashed the tin.

'What's that say? I'm a little nearsighted.'

'It says "Detective",' Meyer answered.

'Yeah?'

'Yeah.'

'Well, what do you want?'

'We want to know the best way to get to Carruthers Street in Calm's Point,' Carella said.

'What?'

'You heard me.'

'I never heard of Carruthers Street.'

'That's because I just made it up,' Carella said.

'Listen, what are you, a bunch of wise guys?' the attendant asked.

'We're two college kids on a scavenger hunt,' Meyer said. 'We're supposed to bring back a hibernating bear, and you're the first one we've seen all day.'

'Haha,' the attendant said mirthlessly. 'That's very funny.'

'What's your name?' Carella asked.

'Quentin. You going to give me trouble? I'm a civil service employee, too, you know. It ain't nice to give your own kind trouble.'

'What's your first name, Mr Quentin?'

'Stan.'

'Stan Quentin?' Meyer asked incredulously.

'Yeah, what's the matter with that?' The old man peered into Meyer's face. 'What's *your* name?'

Meyer, whose full name was Meyer Meyer, the legacy of a practical-joking father, hastily said, 'Let's never mind the names, okay, Mr Quentin? We only want to ask you some questions about what happened downstairs last week, okay?'

'The wop who was killed, you mean?' Quentin asked.

'Yeah, the wop who was killed,' Carella said.

'So what about him? I didn't even know him.'

'Then how do you know he was a wop?'

'I read his name in the papers.' He turned to Meyer again. 'What's wrong with Stan Quentin, would you mind telling me?'

'Nothing. They almost named a prison after you.'

'Yeah? Which one?'

'Alcatraz,' Meyer said.

The old man stared at him blankly. 'I don't get it,' he said.

'Tell us about the day of the murder.'

'There's nothing to tell. The guy downstairs got shot, that's all.'

'He got shot from this platform, Mr Quentin,' Meyer said. 'For all we know, *you* could have done it.'

'Haha,' Quentin said.

'Why not?'

'Why not? Because I can't even read what your shield says from a distance of three feet. How the hell could I shoot a man who's all the way down in the street?'

'You could have used a telescopic sight, Mr Quentin.'

'Sure. I could also be governor of the state.'

'Did you see anyone come onto the platform carrying a rifle?'

'Look,' Quentin said, 'maybe you don't understand me. I don't see too good, you get that? I am the most cockeyed guy you'll ever meet in your life.'

'Then why aren't you wearing glasses?' Carella asked.

'What, and spoil my looks?' Quentin said seriously.

'How do you know how much money a person is giving you?' Meyer asked.

'I hold the bill up to my face.'

'So, let's get this straight, all right? Even if somebody had come up here with a rifle, you wouldn't have seen what he was carrying. Is that what you're saying?'

'I thought I said it pretty plain,' Quentin said. 'What do you mean, Alcatraz? How's that named after me?'

'You work on it, Mr Quentin,' Meyer said. 'Have you got a train schedule here?'

'The company don't issue schedules. You know that.'

'I know the company doesn't, but isn't there one issued to employees? Don't *you* know when the trains come in and out of this platform?'

'Sure I know.'

'Do you think you might be willing to tell us?'

'Sure.'

'When, Mr Quentin? We're sort of anxious to get back to the party.'

'What party?'

'The one we're out on the scavenger hunt from.'

'Haha,' Quentin said.

'So how about it?'

'You want to know every train that comes in and out of here?'

'No. We only want to know the trains that come in and out on the uptown side at about twelve noon. That's what we'd like to know. Do you think you can supply us with the information?'

'I think so,' Quentin said. 'Alcatraz, huh? Where's that?'

'In the water off San Francisco.'

'They made a picture of that once, didn't they?'

'That's right.'

'What'd they do? Use my name in the picture?'

'Why don't you write to the movie company?' Carella suggested.

'I will. Who made the picture?'

'It was an M-G-M musical,' Meyer said.

'Haha,' Quentin said. 'Come on, who made the picture?'

'A couple of convicts,' Carella said. 'It was part of the prison therapy programme.'

'Can I sue a convict?'

'Nope.'

'Then what's the use?'

'There's no use. Just be grateful they named the joint after you, that's all. And as a gesture of your gratefulness, tell us about the trains, okay?'

'You're just a bunch of wise guys,' Quentin said sourly. 'I knew that the minute you came up to the booth.'

'The trains,' Meyer prompted.

'Okay, okay. Weekdays?'

'Weekdays.'

'Around noon?'

'Around noon.'

'There's one gets in at eleven fifty-seven, pulls out about thirty seconds later.'

'And the next one?'

'Gets in at twelve-oh-three.'

'And leaves?'

'Same thing. Thirty seconds or so. They only open the doors, let the people off and on, and shove right off. What do you think this is? A first class coach to Istanbul? This is the elevated system.'

'How are your ears, Mr Quentin?'

'My what?'

'Your ears. Did you hear a shot at about twelve noon on the day Mr Palumbo was killed?'

'What day was that?'

'It was May first.'

'That's only a date. What was the day? I only remember days by days.'

'It was a Tuesday.'

'A week ago?'

'A week ago tomorrow.'

'Nope, I didn't hear no shot on a week ago tomorrow.'

'Thanks, Mr Quentin,' Meyer said. 'You have been extremely helpful.'

'You know those guys at Alcatraz?'

'We know a lot of guys at Alcatraz,' Carella said.

'Tell them to take my name off it, you hear?'

'We will,' Carella said.

'Damn right,' Quentin said.

*

In the street downstairs, Meyer said, 'So?'

'I think our man used a silencer.'

'Me, too.'

'That's a lot of help, isn't it?'

'Oh, yes. Oh my, yes, that's a great deal of help.'

'This case is making me giddy, you know that?'

'You want some coffee?'

'No, spoil my appetite. I want to go see the elevator operator at Norden's apartment building again, and then I want to talk to the woman who witnessed Forrest's death again, and then ...'

'Let's send some of our little helpers.'

'I want to talk to them myself.'

'Why?'

'I don't trust cops,' Carella said, grinning.

*

The young blonde who walked into the squad-room while Bert Kling was poring over the files was Cindy Forrest. She was carrying a black tote bag in one hand and a manila folder under her arm, and she was looking for Detective Steve Carella, ostensibly to give him the material in the folder. Cindy – by her own admission – was a nineteen-year-old girl who would be twenty in June and who had seen it all and heard it all, and also done a little. She thought Steve Carella was an attractive man in a glamour profession – listen, some girls have a thing for cops – and whereas she knew he was married and suspected he had four dozen kids, she nonetheless thought it might be sort of interesting to see him again, the marriage contract being a remote and barely understood cultural curiosity to most nineteen-year-olds going on twenty. She didn't know what would happen with Carella when she saw him again, though she had constructed a rather elaborate fantasy in her own mind and knew exactly what she *wished* would happen. The fact that he was married didn't disturb her at all, nor was she very troubled by the fact that he was almost twice her age. She saw in him a man with an appealing animal vitality, not too dumb for a cop, who had just possibly seen and heard even more than she had, and who had most certainly *done* more than she had, her own experience being limited to once in the back seat of an automobile and another time on a bed at a party in New Ashton. She could remember the names of both boys, but they were only boys, that was the thing, and Steve Carella seemed to her to be a man, which was another thing again and something she felt she ought to experience *now*, before she got married herself one day and tied down with kids.

She hadn't consulted Carella on the possibility as yet, but she felt this was only a minor detail. She was extremely secure in her own good looks and in an undeniable asset called youth. She was certain that once Carella understood her intentions, he would be happy to oblige, and they would then enter into a madly delirious and delicious love affair which would end some months from now because, naturally, it could never be; but Carella would remember her for ever, the nineteen-year-old going on twenty who had shared those tender moments of passion, who had enriched his life, who had rewarded him with her inquiring young mind and her youthful responsive body.

Feeling like Héloïse about to keep an assignation with Abelard, she walked into the squad-room expecting to find Carella – and instead found Bert Kling.

Kling was sitting at his own desk in a shaft of sunlight that came through the grilled window and settled on his blond head like a halo. He was suntanned and muscular, and he was wearing a white shirt open at the throat, and he was bent over the papers spread on his desk, the sun touching his hair, looking very healthy and handsome and young.

She hated him on sight.

'I beg your pardon,' she said.

Kling looked up. 'Yes, miss?'

'I'd like to see Detective Carella, please.'

'Not here right now,' Kling answered. 'Can I help you?'

'Who are *you*?' Cindy asked.

'Detective Kling.'

'How do you do?' She paused. 'You did say *Detective* Kling?'

'That's right.'

'You seem so –' she hesitated on the word, as if it were loathsome to her – 'young. To be a detective, I mean.'

Kling sensed her hostility immediately and immediately reacted in a hostile manner. 'Well, you see,' he said, 'I'm the boss's son. That's how I got to be a detective so fast.'

'Oh, I see.' She looked around the squad-room, obviously annoyed by Kling, and the room, and Carella's absence, and the world. 'When will he be back? Carella?'

'Didn't say. He's out making some calls.'

With a ghoulishly sweet grin, Cindy said, 'And they left *you* to mind the store. How nice.'

'Yeah,' Kling answered, 'they left me to mind the store.' He was not smiling, because he was not enjoying this little snotnose who came up here with her *Saturday Evening Post* face and her college girl talk. 'So since I'm minding the store, what is it you want, miss? I'm busy.'

'Yes, I can see that.'

'What can I do for you?'

'Nothing. I'll wait for Carella, if you don't mind.' She was opening the gate in the slatted rail divider when Kling came out of his chair swiftly and abruptly.

'Hold it right there!' he snapped.

'Wh – what?' Cindy asked, her eyes opening wide.

'Just *hold* it, miss!' Kling shouted, and to Cindy's shocked surprise, he pulled a pistol from a holster clipped to his belt, and pointed it right at her heart.

'Get in here,' he said. 'Don't reach into that bag!'

'What? Are you . . .?'

'*In!*' Kling shouted.

She obeyed him instantly, because she was certain he was going to shoot her dead in the next moment. She had heard stories about cops who lost their minds and went around shooting anything that moved. She was also beginning to wonder whether he really was a cop, and not simply a stray hoodlum who had wandered up here.

'Empty your bag on the desk,' Kling said.

'Listen, what the hell do you think you're . . .?'

'Empty it, miss,' he said menacingly.

'I'm going to *sue* you, you know,' she said coldly, and turned over her bag, spilling the contents onto the desk.

Kling went through the pile of junk rapidly. 'What's in that folder?' he asked.

'Some stuff for Detective Carella.'

'On the desk.'

She put the folder down. Kling loosened the ties on it, and stuck his hand into it. He kept the gun trained at Cindy's middle, and she watched him with growing exasperation.

'All right?' she asked at last.

'Put your hands up over your head as high as you can get them.'

'Listen, I don't have to . . .'

'Miss,' he said warningly, and she raised her hands.

'Higher. Stretch.'

'Why?'

'Because I'd really like to frisk you, but this'll have to do.'

'Oh boy, are you getting in trouble,' she said, and she reached up for the ceiling. He studied her body minutely, looking for the bulge of a gun anywhere under her clothes. He saw only a trim, youthful figure in a white sweater and a straight black skirt. No unexplainable bulges.

'All right, put your hands down. What do you want with Carella?'

'I want to give him what's in that folder. Now suppose you explain...'

'Miss, a couple of years back we had a girl come in here asking for Steve Carella, who happened to be out making a call. None of us could help her. She said she wanted to wait for Steve. So she marched through that gate, just the way you were about to do, and then she pulled out a thirty-eight and the next thing we knew she told us she was here to *kill* Carella.'

'What's that got to do with...?'

'So, miss, I'm only the boss's son and a very dumb cop, but that dame put us through hell for more hours than I care to remember. And I know enough to come in out of the rain. Especially when there's lightning around.'

'I see. And is this what you do with every girl who comes into the squad-room? You frisk them?'

'I didn't frisk you, miss.'

'Are you finished with me?'

'Yes.'

'Then go frisk yourself,' Cindy said, and she turned away from him coldly and began putting the junk back into her bag.

'Let me help you with that,' Kling said.

'Mister, you'd better just stay as far away from me as possible. I don't have a thirty-eight, but if you take one step closer to me I'll clonk you right on the head with my shoe.'

'Look, you weren't exactly radiating...'

'I've never in my entire life dealt with anyone as...'

'... sunshine when you came in here. You looked sore, and I automatically...'

'... suspicious, or as rude, or as overbearing in his manner...'

'... assumed you...'

'Shut up when I'm talking!' Cindy shouted.

'Look, miss,' Kling said angrily. 'This happens to be a police station, and I happen to be a policeman, and I . . .'

'*Some* policeman!' Cindy snapped.

'You want me to kick you out of here?' Kling said menacingly.

'I want you to apologize to me!' Cindy yelled.

'Yeah, you've got a fat chance.'

'Yeah, I'm going to tell you something, Mister Big-shot Boss's Son. If you think a citizen . . .'

'I'm not the boss's son,' Kling yelled.

'You said you were!' Cindy yelled back.

'Only because you were so snotty!'

'*I* was snotty? *I* was . . .'

'I'm not used to seventeen-year-old brats . . .'

'I'm nineteen! Damn you, I'm *twenty*!'

'Make up your mind!' Kling shouted, and Cindy picked up her bag by the straps and swung it at him. Kling instinctively put up one of his hands and the black leather collided with the flat palm, and all the junk Cindy had painstakingly put back into the bag came spilling out again, all over the floor.

They both stood stock still as if the spilling contents of the bag were an avalanche. Cigarettes, matches, lipstick, eyeshadow, sunglasses, a comb, an address and appointment book, a bottle of A.P.C. tablets, a book of 25 gummed parcel-post labels, a cheque-book, a compact, more matches, a package of Chiclets, an empty cigarette package, a scrap of yellow paper with the handwritten words 'Laundry, Quiz Philosophy', a hair-brush, an eyelash curler, two more combs, a package of Kleenex, several soiled Kleenex tissues, more matches, a pillbox without any pills in it, a box of Sucrets, two pencils, a wallet, more matches, a ballpoint pen, three pennies, several empty cellophane wrappers, and a peach pit all came tumbling out of the bag and fell onto the floor to settle in a disorderly heap between them.

Kling looked down at the mess.

Cindy looked down at the mess.

Silently, she knelt and began filling the bag again. She worked without looking up at him, without saying a word. Then she rose, picked up the manila folder from the desk, put it into Kling's hands, and frostily said, 'Will you please see that Detective Carella gets this?'

Kling accepted the folder. 'Who shall I say left it?'

'Cynthia Forrest.'

'Listen, I'm sorry about ...'

'Detective Kling,' Cindy said, enunciating every word sharply and distinctly, 'I think you are the biggest bastard I've ever met in my life.'

Then she turned and walked out of the squad-room.

Kling stared after her a moment, and then shrugged. He carried the manila folder to Carella's desk, remembered abruptly that the name Cynthia Forrest had been in at least two of the D.D. reports he'd read, realized immediately that she was the daughter of the dead Anthony Forrest, almost started out of the squad-room in an attempt to catch up with her, said 'The hell with it,' aloud, and plunked the folder down on Carella's desk-top.

The folder did not contain as much junk as Cindy's bag had contained, but it did hold a great deal of material on the man who had been her father. Most of the stuff dealt with his days as a student at Ramsey University – some of his old term papers, pictures of him with the football squad, several report cards, a notebook he had kept, and, oh, stuff like that. Carella would not see the contents of the folder until the next morning, because he would be occupied uptown all that day, and would go directly home to dinner with his wife and two kids afterwards.

Actually, there wasn't much in the folder that would have helped him or the case. Except perhaps one thing.

The one thing was a frayed and yellowing theatre programme. The front of the programme read:

The Wig and Buskin Society

PRESENTS

THE LONG VOYAGE HOME

A ONE ACT PLAY BY

Eugene O'Neill

The programme sat on top of Carella's desk, inside the manila folder. The inside of the programme listed the past activities of the drama group on the left-hand page, together with a well-wishing half-page ad from the graduating class of June 1940. The back of the programme carried a full-page ad for Harry's Luncheonette, Ice Cream Treats Our Speciality, near the school.

The inside right-hand page of the programme contained the following printed information:

CAST IN ORDER OF APPEARANCE

FAT JOE	*Thomas Di Pasquale*
NICK	*Andrew Mulligan*
MAG	*Margaret Buff*
OLSON	*Randolph Norden*
DRISCOLL	*Anthony Forrest*
COCKY	*David Arthur Cohen*
IVAN	*Peter Kelby*
KATE	*Helen Struthers*
FREDA	*Blanche Ruth Lettiger*
FIRST ROUGH	*Salvatore Palumbo*
SECOND ROUGH	*Rudy Fenstermacher*

That night, while Detective Steve Carella was sitting down to dinner with his wife, Teddy, and the twins, Mark and April, a man named Rudy Fenstermacher was walking from the subway to his home in Majesta.

He never made it, because a .308-calibre bullet hit him right in the head and killed him instantly.

Chapter Twelve

Carella started the next morning by yelling.

He was not a yelling man by nature, and he was very fond of Bert Kling, at whom he was directing his tirade. But he was roaring anyway, so loud that the cops downstairs in the locker room could hear him.

'You call yourself a cop?' he shouted. 'What kind of a cop...'

'I didn't think to look, okay?' Kling said patiently. 'She said it was for you, so...'

'I thought you'd been assigned to this case.'

'That's right,' Kling said patiently.

'Then why didn't...?'

'How the hell was I supposed to know what was in that folder?'

'She gave it to you, didn't she?'

'She said it was for you.'

'So you didn't even look to see what...'

'I *felt* inside it,' Kling said. 'When she first came up.'

'You what?'

'I felt inside it.'

'You *felt*? Did you say "felt"?'

'That's right.'

'What the hell for?'

'To see if she was carrying a gun.'

'Who?'

'Cynthia Forrest.'

'Carrying a *what*?'

'A gun.'

'Cynthia Forrest?'

'Yes.'

'What could have possibly given you the idea that Cynthia Forrest ...'

'Because she came up here asking for you, and when I told her you weren't here, she said she'd wait and then began coming through that gate. And I remembered what happened with Virginia Dodge that time, and I figured maybe this one wanted to put a hole in your head, too. That's why. Okay?'

'Oh boy,' Carella said.

'So I felt in the folder, and I looked in her purse, and when I saw she wasn't heeled, I just took the folder and dumped it on your desk, after I had an argument with her.'

'Without looking inside it.'

'That's right.'

'Oh boy,' Carella said.

'Look, I know I'm just a stupid amateur when it comes to the mastermind ...'

'Cut it out,' Carella said.

'... of the squad, but I'm new on this case, and I don't know who half these people are, and I'm not in the habit of opening something that was specifically ...'

'Go get him a crying towel, will you, Meyer?'

'... left for someone else. Now, if you want to make a big federal case out of this ...'

'*A man was killed last night!*' Carella shouted.

'I know that, Steve,' Kling said. 'But there are a lot of other names on that college programme. And while we're arguing here about what I did or didn't do, our man might be out taking a pot-shot at another one of them.' Kling paused. 'You want to argue, or shall we hit the phone book and try to locate some of the others?'

'For your information, Junior G-man, Meyer and I got to the squad-room at seven o'clock this morning, after spending all night with the family of Rudy Fenstermacher, who was killed last night because ...'

'Steve, get off my back,' Kling said. 'I'm not responsible for what happened last night!'

'Maybe you're not!' Carella shouted.

'No maybe's!'

'Okay! I'm trying to tell you we began checking out the names on that programme the minute I found it on my desk. There were eleven people in that play, and six of them are already dead. Of the remaining five, we've been able to trace only two of the men. The third man isn't listed in the phone book, and the women are probably married, with new names. We've already contacted the university, and they're going to call back if they have any luck. In the meantime, we've called both of the men whose where-abouts are known, and they're expecting our visit. Now, do you think if I gave you a name and address you could find your way to the right house and manage to ask the man some questions about . . .'

'Listen, Steve,' Kling said, 'you're beginning to burn me up, you know that?'

'The man's name is Thomas Di Pasquale. He played Fat Joe in the O'Neill play. His address is four-one-nine Servatius, right here in Isola. He's expecting you.'

'What do you want to know from him?' Kling asked.

'I want to know just what happened back in nineteen forty.'

*

Thomas Di Pasquale lived in a luxurious apartment building on the city's South Side. When Kling rang his doorbell that morning, he shouted, 'Come in, come in, it's open,' and Kling tried the knob and opened the door onto a wide, thickly carpeted entrance foyer, beyond which was a sunken living-room, and a man on a telephone.

The man who had played Fat Joe in a college production years ago was now tall and slim, and somewhat over forty years old. He was wearing a silk dressing-gown and had the telephone to his ear as Kling entered the apartment and closed the door and stood waiting in the foyer. Without looking in Kling's direction, and without stopping his telephone conversation, Di Pasquale gestured to an easy chair opposite him, lighted a cigarette, paused for a moment to allow whoever was on the other end to say something, and then said, 'Hold it, Harry, hold it right there. That's where we stop doing business. There's nothing more to talk about.'

Kling took the seat opposite Di Pasquale, and pretended not to be listening to the conversation.

'No, Harry, but when you start talking in terms of forty G's for someone of this guy's standing and reputation, we got nothing further to say. So if you don't mind, Harry, I'm very busy, and I'm late for the office now, so ...'

Kling lighted a cigarette while Di Pasquale listened for a few seconds. 'Yeah, well then let me hear you *really* talking, Harry. Who? That's a screen writer by you? That's a French fag by me. He can't even speak English, you expect him to do a screenplay about the West? For Chrissake, Harry, make sense.'

He covered the mouthpiece, looked up at Kling, said, 'Hi, there's some coffee in the kitchen, if you want some,' and then immediately said into the phone, 'What do I care if he won the French Academy award? You know what you can do with the French Academy award, don't you? Look, Harry, I'm not interested in who you can get for forty G's. If you want to hire a French fag to write a screenplay about the West, then go right ahead. And good luck to you.' Di Pasquale paused. 'What do you mean, how much am I asking? Make me a sensible offer, for Chrissake! Start around a hundred, and then maybe I'll listen a little.' He covered the mouthpiece again. 'There's coffee in the kitchen,' he said to Kling.

'I've already had breakfast.'

'Well, if you want a cup, there's some in the kitchen. What do you mean, he never got a hundred in his life? He got a hundred and a quarter from Metro the last time out, and the time before that he got a hundred and five from Fox! Now you want to talk, Harry, or you want to waste my time? Well, what is it? Who? Harry, what do I care about Clifford Odets? I don't represent Clifford Odets, and anyway can Clifford Odets write a Western? Well then, fine. If Clifford Odets can write *anything*, then you just go get Clifford Odets. Yeah, and see what *he* costs you! What? No. No, we're starting at a hundred thousand, that's where we start to talk. Well, you think about it, Harry, and give me a ring back. I'll be leaving for the office in a little while. Please, Harry, don't start with the old song and dance again. I don't care if you're gonna have Liz *Taylor* in the picture, which you're not anyway. Stick Liz Taylor in front of the camera without lines to say, and see how long she can ad lib, go ahead. Will you call me back? What? *How* much? Seventy-five? Don't be ridiculous. If I even called him up and told him seventy-five, you know what he'd do? He'd go right over to William Morris tomorrow. That's the truth. I wouldn't insult him. Well, you think about it, I've got company. What? Yeah, yeah, *six* naked blondes, what do you think? We know how to live here in the East. Call me back, baby, huh? I wouldn't steer you wrong, believe me, baby, have I ever sold you a lox? This guy writes like a dream, you could shoot the movie right off the paper it's written on, you don't even need actors, huh, baby? Good, good, I'll hear from you, fine, good-bye, baby, yeah, at the office, so long, sure, baby, think about it, right, good-bye now, yeah, nice talking to you, so long, baby.'

He hung up and turned to Kling.

'Big jerk, he never made a good movie in his life. You want some coffee?'

'Thanks, I've had breakfast.'

'So have a cup of coffee, it'll kill you?'

Di Pasquale turned and walked towards the kitchen. Over his shoulder he said, 'What's your name?'

'Detective Kling,' Kling yelled after him.

'You're a little young to be a detective, ain't you?'

'No, there are men my age who've . . .'

'Where'd you get that tan?' Di Pasquale shouted from the kitchen.

'I was on vacation. Just got back to work yesterday.'

'Looks terrific on you, kid. Blond guys look great with tans. Me, I turn red like a lobster. You take cream and sugar?'

'Yes.'

'All right, I'll bring the works out. Seventy-five grand, he offers. I wasn't kidding him. I call the writer with an offer like that, he'll tell me to go straight to hell.' Di Pasquale came back into the living-room carrying a tray with the coffee-pot, the cups, and the cream and sugar. He put the tray down and said, 'You wouldn't prefer a drink, would you? No, too early in the morning, huh? What the hell time is it, anyway?'

'It's nine-thirty, Mr Di Pasquale.'

'Yeah. You know what time that guy called me? The guy working with you?'

'Carella?'

'Yeah, him. He called me at seven-thirty, the middle of the night! I woke up it was so dark I thought I went blind.' Di Pasquale laughed and poured from the coffee-pot. 'So what's up, kid?'

'Mr Di Pasquale, were you in a play called *The Long Voyage Home* in nineteen forty at Ramsey University in this city?'

'Whaaaat?' Di Pasquale said.

'Were you in a play ...'

'Yeah, yeah, I heard you, but my God, where did you find *that* out? That was before the beginning of time, almost. That was when dinosaurs were still roaming the earth.'

'*Were* you in that play, Mr Di Pasquale?'

'Sure I was. I played Fat Joe, the bartender. I did a pretty good job, too. I wanted to be an actor then, but I was too fat, you see? When I got out of college, I used to go around making my calls, and all the casting directors told me I was too fat. So I went on a crash diet, look at me now, a ninety-seven-pound weakling, people kick sand in my face. But the funny part was, once I slimmed down, I didn't want to be an actor any more. So what am I now? An agent! And I do more acting on that telephone every day of the week than I did all the while I was a professional actor. So what about the play, kid, drink your coffee.'

'Do you remember any of the other people who were in that play, Mr Di Pasquale?'

'Only one, this broad named Helen Struthers. Boy, boy, boy, boy, was she something! Beautiful girl, beautiful. I wonder if she ever made it.'

'Do you remember a man named Anthony Forrest?'

'No.'

'Randolph Norden?'

'Randolph Norden ... yeah, yeah, wait a minute, he played the Swede, yeah, I remember him.'

'Mr Di Pasquale, do you read the newspapers?'

'Sure, I do. *Variety, Hollywood Reporter* ...'

'Any of the dailies?'

'*Hollywood Reporter* is a daily,' Di Pasquale said.

'I meant outside of the trade papers.'

'Sure I do.'

'Mr Di Pasquale, have you read any of the newspaper coverage on the sniper who's killed six people to date?'

'Sure.'

'Do you know that Randolph Norden was ...'

'Oh my God, Randolph Norden!' Di Pasquale said, and he slapped his forehead. 'Holy Jesus, how come it didn't ring a bell? Of course! Of course, for God's sake! He was killed by this nut, wasn't he? So *that's* why you're here. What happened? Who did it?'

'We don't know yet. I mentioned Randolph Norden only because you said you remembered him. But, Mr Di Pasquale, there seems to be a pattern to the killings ...'

'Don't tell me,' Di Pasquale said, and he rolled his eyes towards the ceiling.

'What?'

'He's after all of us who were in the play.'

'We think that's a possibility, sir.'

'I knew it.'

'How did you know it, Mr Di Pasquale?'

'What else could it be? Kid, I been selling stories to the movies since before you could walk. What else could it be? Some nut has taken it in his head to knock off everybody who was in that crummy play. Naturally. It stands to reason. Did he get Helen Struthers yet? Because that would be a real shame, believe me. This was a beautiful girl. Though who knows, she may have grown up to be a beast, huh? Who knows?'

'You don't seem particularly frightened by the idea of ...'

'Frightened? What do you mean?'

'Well, if he's killing everyone who was in that play ...'

'Me? You mean me?'

'You were in the play, Mr Di Pasquale.'

'Yeah, but ...'

'So, you see ...'

'Nah,' Di Pasquale said. He looked at Kling seriously for a moment, and then asked, 'Yeah?'

'Maybe.'

'Pssssss,' Di Pasquale said.

'Do you have any idea who might be doing this, Mr Di Pasquale?'

'Have some more coffee.'

'Thanks.'

'Who could be doing this, huh? Six, you say, huh? Who? Who were the ones killed?'

'Anthony Forrest, I believe you said you didn't know him.'

'No, it doesn't register.'

'Randolph Norden.'

'Yeah.'

'Blanche Lettiger.'

'Blanche Lettiger, no, don't remember her.'

'Salvatore Palumbo.'

'Oh, sure.'

'You know him?'

'Yeah, little Italian immigrant, hot stuff. He was studying English at night session, you know? So he wandered into a rehearsal one night after his class, and it happened we needed somebody for one of the bit parts, I forget which it was. So this little guy who could barely speak English, he took the part. He's supposed to be British, you know? It was a hot sketch, him walking in and talking like a Cockney with an Italian accent a mile long. Funny guy. He got killed, huh? That's too bad. He was a nice little man.' Di Pasquale sighed. 'Who else?'

'A man named Andrew Mulligan.'

'Yeah, I read that. The district attorney. I didn't realize it was the same guy from the play.'

'And last night, a man named Rudy Fenstermacher.'

'That makes five,' Di Pasquale said.

'No, six,' Kling said.

'Norden, right?'

'Yes, and Forrest, and Lettiger ...'

'And the little Italian guy ...'

'Right, that's four. And Mulligan and Fenstermacher. That's six.'

'That's right, six. You're right.'

'Can you tell me a little about the play?'

'We did it in the round,' Di Pasquale said. 'We were all kids, you know how these amateur things are. All of us except the little Italian guy, what was his name?'

'Palumbo.'

'Yeah, he must've been maybe thirty-five years old. But the rest of us were all kids, and I guess the play stunk. I can hardly remember it, tell you the truth. Except for this Helen Struthers who played one of the whores, she wore one of these very low-cut peasant blouses. I wonder what ever happened to her.'

'We're trying to locate her now. You wouldn't know whether she got married, would you? Or left the city?'

'Never saw her before the play, or after it. Oh yeah, maybe in the halls, you know, between classes, hello, good-bye, like that.'

'Did you graduate from Ramsey, Mr Di Pasquale?'

'Sure. I don't sound like a college graduate, do I?'

'You sound fine, sir.'

'Look, you don't have to snow me. I know what I sound like. But the movie business is full of pants pressers. If I sounded like a college graduate, they'd all get nervous. They want me to sound like *I* work in a tailor shop, too. So that's the way I sound.' He shrugged. 'Listen, I can still quote Chaucer, *Whan that Aprille with his shoures sote*, but who wants to hear Chaucer in the movie business? You quote Chaucer in a producer's office, he'll send for the guys in the white jackets. Yeah, I graduated, class of June nineteen forty-two.'

'Were you in the service, Mr Di Pasquale?'

'Nope. Punctured eardrum.'

'Tell me some more about the play.'

'Like what? It was a little college play. We cast it, we rehearsed it, we performed it, we struck it. End of story.'

'Who directed it?'

'The faculty adviser, I forget his na – no, wait a minute. Richardson. Professor Richardson, that was it. Boy, the things you remember, huh? This was more than twenty years ago.' Di Pasquale paused. 'You sure somebody's trying to ...' He shrugged. 'You know, twenty years is a long, long time. I mean, like man, that has to be one hell of a grudge to carry for twenty years.'

'Was there any trouble during rehearsals, sir, would you remember?'

'Oh, the usual junk. You know actors. Even the pros are disgusting, all ego and a mile high. Well, amateurs are worse. But I can't remember any big fight or anything like that. Nothing that would last twenty years.'

'How about Professor Richardson? Did everyone in the cast get along with him?'

'Yeah, a harmless guy. Nothing on the ball, but harmless.'

'Then you can't remember anything that might have caused this kind of extreme reaction.'

'Nothing.' Di Pasquale paused reflectively. 'You think this guy is *really* out to get all of us?'

'We're going on that assumption, Mr Di Pasquale.'

'So where does that leave me? Do I get police protection?'

'If you want it.'

'I want it.'

'You'll get it.'

'Pssssss,' Di Pasquale said.

'There's just one other thing, Mr Di Pasquale,' Kling said.

'Yeah, I know. Don't leave town.'

Kling smiled. 'That's just what I was going to say.'

'Sure, what else could you say? I've been in this movie business a long time, kid. I've read them all, I've seen them all. It don't take too much brains to figure it.'

'To figure what?'

'That if somebody's out to get all of us who were in the play, well, kid, figure it. The somebody who's out to get us *could* be somebody who was in the play, too. Right? So, okay, I won't leave town. When are you sending the protection?'

'I'll get a patrolman here within the half-hour. I should tell you, Mr Di Pasquale, that so far the killer has struck without warning and from a distance. I'm not sure what good our protection will . . .'

'Anything's better than nothing,' Di Pasquale said. 'Look, baby, you finished with me?'

'Yes, I think . . .'

'Well then, good, kid,' he said, leading him to the door. 'If you don't mind, I'm in a hell of a hurry. That guy's gonna call me back at the office, baby, and I've got a million things on my desk, so thanks for coming up and talking to me, huh? I'll be looking for the cop, kid. send him over right away before I'm gone, huh, baby? Good, it was nice seeing you, take it easy, baby, so long. huh?'

And the door closed behind Kling.

Chapter Thirteen

David Arthur Cohen was a sour little man who made his living
being funny.

He operated out of a one-room office on the fourteenth floor
of a building on Jefferson, and it was in this office that he greeted
the detectives sourly, offered them chairs sourly, and then said,
'It's about these killings, isn't it?'

'That's right, Mr Cohen,' Meyer said.

Cohen nodded. He was a thin man with a pained and suffering
look in his brown eyes. He was almost as bald as Meyer, and the
two men, sitting on opposite sides of the desk, with Carella
standing between them at one end of the desk, looked like a pair
of billiard balls waiting for a careful shooter to decide how he
would bank them.

'It dawned on me when Mulligan was murdered,' Cohen said.
'I'd recognized the other names before then, but when Mulligan
got killed, the whole thing suddenly fell into place. I realized he
was after all of us.'

'You realized this when Mulligan was killed, huh?' Meyer
said.

'That's right.'

'Mulligan was killed on May second, Mr Cohen. This is May
eighth.'

'That's right.'

'That's almost a full week, Mr Cohen.'

'I know that.'

'Why didn't you call the police?'

'What for?'

'To tell us what you suspected.'

'I'm a busy man.'

'We understand that,' Carella said. 'But surely you're not too
busy to bother trying to save your own life, are you?'

'Nobody's going to shoot me,' Cohen said.

'No. You have a guarantee of that?'

'Did you guys come up here to argue? I'm too busy to argue.'

'Why didn't you call us, Mr Cohen?'

'I told you. I'm busy.'

'What do you do, Mr Cohen? What makes you so busy?'

'I'm a gag-writer.'

'What do you mean?'

'I write gags.'

'For what? For whom?'

'For cartoonists.'

'Comic strips?'

'No, no, single-box stuff. Like you see in the magazines. I write captions for them.'

'Let me get this straight, Mr Cohen,' Carella said. 'You work with a cartoonist who ...'

'I work with a *lot* of cartoonists.'

'All right, you work with a lot of cartoonists who send you drawings to which you write captions? Is that it?'

'No. I send them the caption, and they make the drawing.'

'From the caption?'

'From a lot more than the caption.'

'I still don't understand.'

'Do you see these filing-cabinets?' Cohen asked, waving his arm towards the wall behind him. 'They're full of cartoon ideas. I write up the gag, and then I send a batch of them to any one of the cartoonists on my list. They read the gags. If they like four, or five, or even one, they'll hold it and draw up a rough sketch to show the humour editor of the magazine or newspaper. If the editor okays it, the cartoonist draws up a finish, gets his cheque, and sends me my cut.'

'How much is your cut?'

'I get ten per cent of the purchase price.' Cohen looked at the detectives, saw that they were still puzzled, and said, 'Here, let me show you.' He turned in his swivel chair, opened one of the files at random, and pulled out a thick sheaf of small white slips measuring about three by five. 'There's a gag typed on each one of these slips,' Cohen said. 'See? That's the number in the right-hand corner – each gag has a different number – and my name on the bottom of the slip.' He spread several of the slips on the desk-top. Meyer and Carella leaned over the desk and read the nearest one.

```
                                          #702

   A picket on strike outside the Excelsior Match
   Company is being stopped by a passer-by.  The
   passer-by says:

   "Got a match, buddy?"

                              David Arthur Cohen
                              1142 Jefferson Avenue
                              Isola
```

'That's what you send the cartoonist?' Carella asked.
'Yeah,' Cohen said. 'Here's a good one. Look at this one.'
Carella looked.

```
                                          #708

   A barroom.  Two men are having a violent fist
   fight.  In the background are the usual men
   standing at the bar.  They are all watching a
   fight on the television set.

   No caption.

                              David Arthur Cohen
                              1142 Jefferson Avenue
                              Isola
```

'That's pretty funny,' Meyer said.
Cohen nodded sourly. 'Here's the one right after it. This is called snowballing. You write one gag, and another one along

similar lines suggests itself, and you write that one. Here, look
at it.'

```
                                              #709

    Cleanup woman in television studio standing
    with surprised look on her face. She is watch-
    ing a television set and the picture is one of
    her cleaning up the studio.


    No caption.


                        David Arthur Cohen
                        1142 Jefferson Avenue
                        Isola
```

'I don't get it,' Meyer said.
'Well, you either get them or you don't,' Cohen answered,
shrugging. 'Here's one of my favourites.'

```
                                              #712

    Car with a telephone.  On the back seat, a drunk
    in a tuxedo is sprawled out, dead to the world.
    Chauffeur, speaking into phone, says:


    "He's out just now.  Can you call later?"


                        David Arthur Cohen
                        1142 Jefferson Avenue
                        Isola
```

'Is this what you do all day long?' Carella asked.
'All day long,' Cohen said.
'How many of these do you write every day?'
'It depends on how it's going,' Cohen answered. 'Sometimes
I can turn out twenty or thirty a day. Other times I'll just sit at the
typewriter, and nothing'll come to mind at all. It runs in cycles.'

'Do all cartoonists use gag-writers?'

'Not all of them. But a great many. I send to about a dozen of them regularly. I've got ... oh ... maybe two hundred gags at market right this minute. I mean, gags they've held and drawn up to show around. I make a pretty good living at it.'

'I'd go out of my mind,' Meyer said.

'Well, it's not bad, really it isn't,' Cohen said.

'Do you enjoy doing it?' Carella asked.

For a moment, the three men had forgotten why they were in that office. They were in that office to discuss six murders, but for the moment Cohen was a professional explaining his craft, and Meyer and Carella were two quite different professionals who were fascinated by the details of another man's work.

'Sometimes it gets a little dull,' Cohen said. 'When the ideas aren't coming. But I usually enjoy it, yes.'

'Do your jokes make *you* laugh?' Carella asked.

'Hardly ever.'

'Then how do you know whether they're funny or not?'

'I don't. I just write them and hope somebody else'll think they're funny.' He shrugged. 'I guess they must be, because I sell an awful lot of them. To the best magazines, too.'

'I never met a gag-writer before,' Meyer said, cocking his head to one side appreciatively.

'I never met a detective before,' Cohen said, and suddenly the visit came back into focus, suddenly there were two detectives in a small office with a man who was linked to six homicides. In deference to the pleasant tangent, there were perhaps thirty seconds of silence. Then Meyer said, 'Can you tell us anything about that play in nineteen forty, Mr Cohen?'

'There isn't much to tell,' Cohen said. 'I went into it for kicks. I was a liberal arts major, and I hadn't yet made up my mind what I wanted to do, so I was experimenting. I fooled around with the drama group for about a year, I guess.'

'Acting?'

'Acting, yes, and I also wrote some skits for a revue we did.'

'When was that?'

'After *The Long Voyage Home*; nineteen forty-one, I think.'

'What about the people who were in the O'Neill play? What do you remember about them?'

'Gee, that was a long time ago,' Cohen said.

'Was there anything out of line? An incident of some kind? A fight? Even a heated argument?'

'Not that I can recall. It seemed like a pretty smooth production. I think everyone got along pretty well.'

'There were three girls in the play,' Carella said. 'Was there any trouble with them?'

'What kind of trouble?'

'Two guys falling for the same girl, anything like that?'

'No, nothing,' Cohen said.

'Then nothing out of the ordinary happened?'

'I can't remember anything. It was just a routine college show. We all got along pretty well.' Cohen hesitated. 'Even had a party after the show.'

'Anything out of line happen at the party?'

'No.'

'Who was there?'

'The cast, and the crew, and Professor Richardson, the faculty adviser. He left early.'

'How late did you stay?'

'Until it was over.'

'And when was that?'

'Oh, I don't remember. Early in the morning sometime.'

'Who else was there when it broke up?'

'Five or six of us.' Cohen shrugged. 'Six, I guess.'

'Who were the six?'

'Three guys and three girls.'

'Who were the girls?'

'The three who were in the show. Helen Struthers, and the other two.'

'And the guys?'

'Tony Forrest, Randy Norden, and me.'

'Any trouble?'

'No. Look, we were kids. We were all in separate rooms, necking.'

'And then what, Mr Cohen?'

'Then we all went home.'

'All right, what'd you do after you got out of college? Were you in the service?'

'Yes.'

'What branch?'

'The army. The infantry.'

'What was your rank?'

'I was a corporal.'

'And your job?'

Cohen hesitated. 'I . . .' He shrugged. 'I told you. I was in the infantry.'

'What'd you do in the infantry?'

'I was a sniper,' Cohen said.

The room went silent.

'I know how that sounds.'

'How does it sound, Mr Cohen?'

'Well, I'm not exactly an idiot, and I know the man who's been doing these killings is a . . . a sniper.'

'Yes, that's right.'

'I haven't seen a rifle since I was discharged in nineteen forty-six,' Cohen said. 'I never want to see another rifle as long as I live.'

'Why?'

'Because I didn't like killing people from ambush.'

'But you were an expert marksman, is that right?'

'Yes.'

'Do you shoot at all now?'

'I told you . . .'

'Hunting, I mean. For sport.'

'No.'

'Do you own a rifle, Mr Cohen?'

'No.'

'A pistol?'

'No.'

'Any kind of a weapon?'

'No.'

'Have you ever used a telescopic sight?'

'Yes, in the army.' Cohen paused. 'You're barking up the wrong tree,' he said. 'Nowadays, when I talk about killing somebody, I mean I've written a gag that'll knock him dead.'

'And that's all you mean?'

'That's all.'

'Mr Cohen,' Meyer said, 'where do you live?'

'Uptown. Near the Coliseum.'

'We'd like to take a look at your apartment, Mr Cohen, if that's all right with you.'

'And if it isn't?'

'We'll be forced to swear out a search warrant.'

Cohen reached into his pocket and threw a ring of keys on the desk. 'I've got nothing to hide,' he said. 'The key with the round head opens the vestibule door. The brass key opens the apartment door.'

'The address?'

'One hundred and twenty-seven North Garrod.'

'And the apartment number?'

'Four C.'

'We'll give you a receipt for the keys, Mr Cohen,' Carella said.

'Will you be out of there by six?' Cohen asked. 'I've got a date.'

'I imagine so. We appreciate your co-operation.'

'I just have one question,' Cohen said. 'If this guy *is* out to get us, how do I know I'm not next?'

'Would you like police protection?' Carella asked. 'We can provide it, if you like.'

'What kind of protection?'

'A patrolman.'

Cohen considered this for a moment. Then he said, 'Forget it. There's no protection against a sniper. I used to be one.'

*

In the street outside, Carella asked, 'What do you think?'

'I think he's clean,' Meyer said.

'Why?'

'Well, I'll tell you. I've been watching television, and going to the movies, and reading books, and I discovered something about homicide.'

'What's that?'

'If there's a Jew, or an Italian, or a Negro, or a Puerto Rican, or a guy with any foreign-sounding name he's never the one who did it.'

'Why not?'

'It ain't permitted, that's why. The killer has to be a hunnerd-percent white American Protestant. I'll bet you ten bucks we don't find anything bigger than a slingshot in Cohen's apartment.'

Chapter Fourteen

```
                                            #1841

   A detective squadroom.  Two detectives are sit-
   ting on opposite sides of a desk, looking through
   the window at the beautiful May sunshine out-
   side.  A big black bomb is on the desk, and the
   fuse is burning furiously, but neither of the
   detectives sees it.  One of them says:

   "It's hard to think about crime on a day like
   this, isn't it?"


                          David Arthur Cohen
                          1142 Jefferson Avenue
                          Isola
```

The big black bomb with the furiously burning fuse was an unknown sniper somewhere out there in a city of ten million people. The two detectives sitting in a shoddy detective squadroom were drinking coffee from cardboard containers and looking out at the May sunshine streaming through the grilled window. They had searched David Arthur Cohen's apartment from transom to trellis – the apartment boasted a small outdoor terrace overlooking a beautiful view of the River Harb – and found nothing at all incriminating. This did not mean that Cohen wasn't a very clever murderer who had hidden his rifle in an old garage somewhere. It simply meant that, for the time being, the detectives had found nothing in his apartment.

At three-thirty that afternoon, long after they had returned Cohen's keys to him, the telephone on Carella's desk rang, and he picked the receiver from its cradle and said, 'Eighty-seventh Squad, Carella.'

'Mr Carella, this is Agnes Moriarty.'

'Hello, Miss Moriarty. How are you?'

'Fine, thank you. Suffering a bit of eyestrain, but all right otherwise.'

'Did you find anything?'

'Mr Carella, I've been searching through our files since you called this morning. I am a very weary woman.'

'We certainly appreciate your help,' Carella said.

'Well, don't get too appreciative until I tell you what I've found.'

'What's that, Miss Moriarty?'

'Nothing.'

'Oh.' Carella paused. 'Nothing at all?'

'Well, *next* to nothing, anyway. I couldn't find the slightest bit of information on the two girls. I had home addresses for both of them here in the city, but that was twenty-three years ago, Mr Carella, and when I called the numbers, the people who answered had never heard of Margaret Buff or Helen Struthers.'

'That's understandable,' Carella said.

'Yes,' Miss Moriarty answered. 'Then I called Mrs Finch, who heads our alumni association, and asked her if *she* had any information on them. Apparently they had both come back to the college for the five-year reunion, but neither was married at the time, and they dropped out of the association shortly thereafter.' Miss Moriarty paused. 'Reunions can be very frightening things, you know.'

'Did she know whether or not they're married now?'

'She had not heard from either of them since that reunion.'

'Well, that's too bad,' Carella said.

'Yes. I'm sorry.'

'What about the man? Peter Kelby.'

'Again, I went over his records with a fine-tooth comb, and I called the phone number he had listed, and I spoke to a very irate man who told me he worked nights and didn't like being awakened by a maiden lady in the middle of the day. I asked him if he was Peter Kelby, and he said he was Irving Dreyfus, if that means anything to you.'

'Nothing at all.'

'He said he had never heard of Peter Kelby, which didn't surprise me in the least.'

'What did you do then?'

'I called Mrs Finch. Mrs Finch went through her records, and called back to tell me that apparently Peter Kelby had never graduated from Ramsey and therefore she could find nothing on him as an alumnus. I thanked her very much, and hung up, and then went back to my own records again. Mrs Finch was right, and I chastised myself for having missed the fact that Peter Kelby dropped out of school in his junior year.'

'So you got nothing on him either, is that it?'

'Well, I'm a very persevering woman, Mr Carella. For a maiden lady, that is. I discovered that Peter Kelby had been a member of a fraternity called Kappa Kappa Delta, and I called the local chapter and asked them whether or not they knew anything about his current whereabouts, and they referred me to the national chapter, and I called them, and the last known address they had for Peter Kelby was one he registered with them in nineteen fifty-seven.'

'Where?'

'Minneapolis, Minnesota.'

'Did you try to reach him there?'

'I'm afraid the school authorities would have frowned upon a long-distance call, Mr Carella. But I do have the address, and I will give it to you if you promise me one thing.'

'What's that, Miss Moriarty?'

'I want you to promise that if I ever get a speeding ticket, you'll fix it for me.'

'Why, Miss Moriarty!' Carella said. 'Don't tell me you're a speeder!'

'Would I admit something like that to a cop?' Miss Moriarty asked. 'I'm waiting for you to promise.'

'What makes you think I can fix a ticket?'

'I have heard it bruited about that one can fix anything but narcotics or homicide in this city.'

'And do you believe that?'

'Assault costs a hundred dollars on the line, I've been told. Burglary can be fixed for five hundred.'

'Where do you get your information, Miss Moriarty?'

'For a maiden lady,' Miss Moriarty said, 'I get around.'

'I can arrest you for attempting to bribe an officer, and also for withholding information,' Carella said, smiling.

'What information? I don't know what you're talking about.'

'Peter Kelby's last known address.'

'Who's Peter Kelby?' Miss Moriarty said, and Carella burst out laughing.

'Okay, okay,' he said, 'you've got my promise. No guarantees, you understand, but I'll certainly try . . .'

'Have you got a pencil?' Miss Moriarty asked.

*

The telephone operator supplied Carella with a number listed to the address of Peter Kelby in Minneapolis, Minnesota. He asked her if she would try the number for him, and then he listened to a series of clickings and bongs and chimes on the line, and finally he heard the phone ringing on the other end, lo, those many miles away, and then a woman answered the phone and said, 'Kelby residence.'

'May I speak to Mr Kelby, please?' Carella said.

'Who's calling, please?' the voice asked.

'Detective Stephen Carella.'

'Just a minute, please.'

Carella waited. He could hear a voice calling to someone on the other end, and then he heard someone asking 'Who?' and the original voice saying, 'A *Detective* Carella,' and then the sound of footsteps approaching the phone, and the sound of the phone being lifted from the table-top, and then a different woman's voice saying, 'Hello?'

'Hello,' Carella said. 'This is Detective Carella of the Eighty-seventh Squad in Isola. I'm calling . . .'

'Yes? This is Mrs Kelby speaking.'

'Mrs *Peter* Kelby?'

'Yes, that's right. What is it?'

'May I speak to your husband, please, Mrs Kelby?' Carella said.

135

There was a long pause on the line.

'Mrs Kelby?'

'Yes?'

'May I . . .'

'Yes, I heard you.'

There was another pause.

Then Mrs Kelby said, 'My husband is dead.'

        *

Which, of course, explained only one thing.

Peter Kelby had been shot to death on May 4. He had been killed while driving to the country club for a drink, as was his habit, after a long week of labour in the insurance office he headed. The Remington .308 slug had smashed through the windshield and entered his throat, and the automobile had swerved out of control and hit a milk-truck going in the opposite direction. Peter Kelby was dead before the vehicles struck each other. But the murderer now had a few residual benefits to his credit, since there were two men in the cab of the milk-truck and when Kelby's car hit it, one of the men went through the windshield and had his jugular severed by a shard of glass, and the other wrenched at the wheel in an attempt to keep the truck on the road, and suddenly discovered that the steering-shaft was pushing up into his chest. That was the last discovery he ever made because he was dead within the next ten seconds.

The three deaths explained only one thing.

They explained why there had been no murders in the city between May 2, when Andrew Mulligan was killed, and May 7, when Rudy Fenstermacher was killed.

It is very difficult for someone to be in two places at the same time.

        *

The woman walked into the squad-room at exactly 5.37, just as Carella and Meyer were leaving for home. Carella was in the middle of a sentence containing a choice bit of profanity, the words, 'Now why the f– ' stopping immediately in his throat when the woman appeared at the slatted rail divider.

She was a tall redhead, with a creamy pale complexion and

slanted green eyes. She wore a dark green suit that captured the colour of her eyes and captured, too, the mould of her body, classically rounded, narrow-waisted, wide-hipped. She was pushing forty, but there was contained voluptuousness in the woman who stood at the railing, and Meyer and Carella – both married men – caught their breath for an instant, as though a fantasy had suddenly materialized. Down the corridor, and behind the woman, Miscolo – who had caught a glimpse of her as she passed his open door – peeked around the jamb of the Clerical Office for a better look, and then rolled his eyes towards the ceiling.

'Yes, miss?' Carella said.

'I'm Helen Vale,' she said.

'Yes, Miss Vale?' Carella said. 'What can we do for you?'

'*Mrs* Vale,' she corrected.

'Yes, Mrs Vale?'

'Helen *Struthers* Vale.'

She spoke in a normally deep voice that carried the unmistakable stamp of elocution lessons. She kept both hands on the slatted rail divider, clinging to it as if it were a lover. She waited patiently, as though embarrassed by her surroundings and embarrassed, too, by the mature ripeness of her own body. And yet, her own awareness seemed to heighten the awareness of the observer. She was a potential rape victim expecting the worst, and inviting it through dire expectation. It took several seconds for the detectives to extract the maiden name 'Struthers' from the names fore and aft, and then to separate it from the heavy miasma of sensuality that had suddenly smothered the room.

'Come in, Mrs Vale,' Carella said, and he held open the gate in the railing for her.

'Thank you,' she said. She lowered her eyes as she passed him, like a novice nun who has reluctantly taken a belated vow of chastity. Meyer pulled a chair out from one of the desks and held it for her while she sat. She crossed her legs, her skirt was short, it rode up over splendid knees, she tugged at it but it refused to yield, she sat in bursting provocative awareness.

Meyer wiped his brow.

'We've been trying to locate you, Mrs Vale,' Carella said. 'You *are* the Helen Struthers who . . .'

'Yes,' she said.

'We assumed you were married, but we didn't know to whom, and we had no idea where to begin looking because this is a very large city, and although we tried ...' He abruptly stopped speaking, wondering why he was talking so rapidly and so much.

'Anyway, we're glad you're here,' Meyer said.

Carella wiped his brow.

'Yes, I thought I should come,' Helen said, 'and now I'm glad I did.' She delivered these last words as if she were paying tribute to the two most handsome, charming, gallant, intelligent men in the world. Both detectives smiled unconsciously and then, catching the smile on the other's face, frowned and tried to become businesslike.

'Why *did* you come, Mrs Vale?' Carella said.

'Well ... because of the shootings,' Helen answered, opening her eyes wide.

'Yes, what about them?'

'He's killing everyone in the play, don't you see?' she said.

'*Who* is, Mrs Vale?'

'Well, I don't know,' she said, and she lowered her eyes again, and again tugged at her skirt, but her skirt didn't budge. 'I thought so at first when I connected the names Forrest and Norden, but then I thought, "No, Helen, you're imagining things." I have a very good imagination,' she explained, raising her eyes.

'Yes, Mrs Vale, go on.'

'Then the girl got killed, I forget her name, and then Sal Palumbo, the nice Italian man who was studying English in night school, and then Andy Mulligan, and Rudy, and I knew for certain. I said to my husband: "Alec, somebody's killing everyone who was in *The Long Voyage Home* in nineteen forty at Ramsey University." That's what I said.'

'And what did your husband say?'

'He said, "You're crazy, Helen."'

'I see.'

'Crazy like a fox,' Helen said, her eyes narrowing. 'So I decided to come up here.'

'Why? Do you have some information for us, Mrs Vale?'

'No,' Helen wet her lips. 'I'm an actress, you see.'

'I see.'

'Yes. Helen Vale. Do you think Struthers would be better?'

'I beg your pardon?'

'Helen Struthers. My maiden name. Does that sound better?'

'Well, no, this is fine.'

'Helen Vale sounds very good,' Meyer agreed, nodding.

'Pure,' she said. 'Classical.'

'What?'

'Helen. It sounds pure and classical.'

'Yes, it does.'

'And Vale adds mystery, don't you think? Vale. V-A-L-E. Which is my husband's real name. But it can also be spelled V-E-I-L, which is what gives it the mystery. Helen Vale. A veil is very mysterious, you know.'

'It certainly is.'

'Being an actress, I decided I should come up here.'

'Why?'

'Well, what good is a dead actress?' Helen said. She shrugged and then spread her hands in utter simplicity.

'That's true,' Meyer said.

'So here I am.'

'Yes,' Carella said.

Miscolo sauntered casually into the squad-room and said, 'Anybody want some coffee? Oh, excuse me, I didn't know you had a visitor.' He smiled graciously at Helen, and she returned the smile demurely and tugged at her skirt. 'Would you like some coffee, miss?' he asked.

'No, thank you,' she said. 'But thank you for asking.'

'Not at all,' Miscolo said, and he went out of the squad-room humming.

'I almost married a man named Leach,' Helen said. 'Helen Leach, wouldn't that have been terrible?'

'Awful,' Meyer agreed.

'Still, he was a nice fellow.'

'Miss Lea ... Miss ... uh ... Mrs Vale,' Carella said, 'what do you remember about *The Long Voyage Home*?'

'I played Kate,' she said. She smiled.

'What else do you remember about it?'

'Nothing.'

'Nothing at all?'

'It was lousy, I think. I don't remember.'

'What do you remember about the other people in the cast?'

'The boys were all very sweet.'

'And the girls?'

'I don't remember them.'

'Would you happen to know whether Margaret Buff ever married?'

'Margaret *who*?'

'Buff. She was in the play, too.'

'No, I don't remember her.'

Two patrolmen wandered into the squad-room, went to the files, opened them, looked at Helen Vale where she sat with her legs crossed, and then went to the water-cooler where they drank three cups of water each while watching Helen Vale where she sat with her legs crossed. As they were leaving the squad-room, four more patrolmen wandered into the room. Carella frowned at them, but they all went about finding busy-work that only happened to take Helen into their direct line of view.

'Have you been an actress ever since you got out of college, Mrs Vale?' Carella asked.

'Yes.'

'Have you appeared on the stage here in this city?'

'Yes. I'm Equity, and AFTRA, and also SAG.'

'Mrs Vale, has anyone ever made any threats on your life?'

'No.' Helen frowned. 'That's a very funny question. What's this got to do with me alone, if the killer is after *all* of us?'

'Mrs Vale, the wholesale slaughter may be just a smoke-screen. He may be after *one* of you, and he may be killing the others to throw us off the track, to make it seem he has a different motive, other than what may be the real motive.'

'Really?'

'Yes,' Carella said.

'I didn't understand a word of that,' Helen said.

'Oh. Well, you see . . .'

'Besides, that's not what interests me. I mean, his motives or anything.'

There were fourteen patrolmen in the room now, and the word was spreading throughout the building, and perhaps the entire precinct, very rapidly. Only once during his entire career as a detective could Carella remember seeing so many patrolmen in the squad-room at one time, and that was when the commissioner had issued his edict against moonlighting, and every uniformed cop in the precinct had come upstairs to bellyache about it in a sort of open forum.

'What *does* interest you, Mrs Vale?' he asked, and five more patrolmen came down the corridor and into the room.

'I think I need protection,' she said, and she lowered her eyes at that moment, as if she were talking not about the sniper who was going around shooting people, but about the patrolmen who were crowding into the room like migrating sardines.

Carella stood up suddenly and said, 'Fellows, it's getting a little stuffy in here Why don't you go have your meeting in the locker room?'

'What meeting?' one of the patrolmen asked.

'The meeting you're going to have in the locker room in three seconds flat,' Carella said, 'before I pick up the phone and have a talk with Captain Frick downstairs.'

The patrolmen began to disperse. One of them, in a very loud *sotto voce*, muttered the word 'Chicken', but Carella ignored it. He watched them as they left, and then he turned to Helen and said, 'We'll assign a man to you, Mrs Vale.'

'I *would* appreciate that,' she said. 'Who?'

'Well ... I'm not sure yet. It depends on who's available and what ...'

'I'm sure he'll be dependable,' she said.

'Mrs Vale,' Carella said, 'I wonder if you can try remembering about the play. I know it was a long time ago, but ...'

'Actually, I have a very good memory,' Helen said.

'I'm sure you do.'

'Actresses *need* to have good memories, you know.'

'I know that.'

'Otherwise we'd never learn our lines,' Helen said, and she smiled.

'Good. What do you remember about the play?'

'Nothing,' Helen said.

'Everyone got along fine with each other, is that right?' Carella prodded.

'Oh yes, it was a very nice group.'

'At the party, too, right? No trouble?'

'Oh no, it was a lovely party.'

'You stayed late, is that right?'

'That's right.' Helen smiled. 'I always stay late at parties.'

'Where was this party, Mrs Vale?'

'What party?' Helen asked.

'The one after the play.'

'Oh, that one. At Randy's house, I think. Randy Norden. He was a regular rip. Very smart in school, you know, but oh what a rip! His parents were away in Europe, so we all went up there after the show.'

'And you and the other two girls stayed late, is that right?'

'That's right, yes. It was a lovely party.'

'With three of the boys.'

'Oh no, there were a lot of boys.'

'I meant you stayed late. With three of the boys.'

'Oh. Yes, that's right. We did.'

'Was there any trouble?'

'No,' Helen said. She smiled sweetly. 'We were making love.'

'You were necking, you mean.'

'No, no. We were diddling.'

Carella cleared his throat and looked at Meyer.

'It was a very nice party,' Helen said.

'Mrs Vale,' Carella said, 'what do you mean by "diddling"?'

Helen lowered her eyes. 'Well you know,' she said.

Carella looked at Meyer again. Meyer shrugged in confusion.

'With the boys, do you mean? The three boys?'

'Yes.'

'You . . . you were in separate rooms, is that right?'

'Yes. Well, in the beginning, anyway. There was an awful lot to drink, you know, and Randy's parents were in Europe, so we just had a lot of fun.'

'Mrs Vale,' Carella said, taking the bull by the horns, 'do you mean that you and the other two girls were *intimate* with these boys?'

'Oh yes, very intimate,' she said.

'And the three boys were Anthony Forrest, Randolph Norden, and David Arthur Cohen, is that right?'

'That's right. They were all very nice boys.'

'And you ... you were sort of wandering around from room to room, is that right? All of you?'

'Oh yes,' Helen said delightedly. 'It was a regular orgy.'

Carella began coughing, and Meyer hit him on the back.

'You're coming down with something,' Helen said pleasantly. 'You ought to get to bed.'

'Yes, yes, I will,' Carella said, coughing. 'Thank you very much, Mrs Vale, you've been very helpful.'

'Oh, I enjoyed talking with you,' Helen said. 'I'd almost forgotten that party, and it was really one of the nicest parties I've ever been to.'

She rose, picked up her purse, opened it, and placed a small white card on the desk. 'My home address and number,' she said, 'and also my service, if you can't reach me.'

She smiled and walking to the railing. Carella and Meyer sat rooted to the desk, watching her move across the room. At the railing, she turned and said, 'You *will* do your best to see that I'm not killed, won't you?'

'We will, Mrs Vale,' Carella said fervently. 'We most certainly will do our very utmost best.'

'Thank you,' she murmured, and then walked down the corridor. They could hear her high heels clattering on the iron-runged steps to the floor below.

'Because, lady,' Meyer whispered, 'it would be a *crime* to kill you, I swear to God, it would be a heinous crime.'

They knew when she reached the street outside because a tumultuous cheer went up from the patrolmen waiting there for her.

Chapter Fifteen

Well, things were certainly looking up.

Not only did they now know that the seven murder victims had all been in a college production of *The Long Voyage Home* back in 1940, but they further knew there had been a party after the play, and that all the members of the cast and crew had been present at it, as well as Professor Richardson, the faculty adviser. They further knew that the faculty adviser had stopped advising some time during the night, and that the party had dwindled down to six people of opposite sexes who had taken advantage of the fact.

The next morning, they decided to have another chat with David Arthur Cohen who, by his own admission, had been a sniper during the war, and who had also been present at the midnight revelry those many years ago. They called him and asked him to come up to the squad-room. He complained bitterly because he said he'd lose a whole day's work in a week when the gags were coming fast and good, but they told him this happened to be a homicide case and if he came to the squad-room of his own volition, it would save them the trouble of sending a patrolman after him.

Cohen arrived at 10 a.m.

They sat him in a chair, and then they stood around him, Kling, Carella, and Meyer. Cohen was rushing the season a bit with a seersucker suit. He looked cool and unruffled. He sat in the chair with his habitual sour expression, and waited for one of the detectives to start the questioning. Meyer threw the first pitch.

'We're primarily interested in the party that took place after the play, Mr Cohen,' he said.

'Yeah, what about it?'

'We want to know what happened.'

'I told you what happened.'

'All right, Mr Cohen,' Carella said, 'first of all, who was there?'

'Everybody in the show.'

'*In* the show, or *connected* with the show?'

'Connected with it.'

'And by "everybody", who exactly do you mean?'

'The cast, the crew, and some hangers-on.'

'Like who?'

'Like some guys brought girls, and also some of the kids who weren't really in the group, but who were on the fringes of it.'

'And who else?'

'Professor Richardson.'

'Was it a good party?' Kling asked.

'Yeah, it was okay. This was more than twenty years ago, for God's sake. Do you expect me to remember . . .'

'Helen Struthers was in here yesterday, Mr Cohen,' Meyer said. 'She seems to remember the party pretty well.'

'Oh yeah?'

'Yeah. She says it was one of the best parties she'd ever been to. How about it?'

'She's entitled to her opinion, I guess.' Cohen paused. 'How'd she look? Helen?'

'Very nice. How was the party in your opinion, Mr Cohen?'

'Pretty good.'

'Helen seemed to think it was better than pretty good,' Carella said.

'Yeah?'

'Yeah. She seemed especially to remember what happened after most of the people went home.'

'Yeah? What does she remember?'

'Well, what do *you* remember, Mr Cohen?'

'We were necking around a little.'

'That's all?'

'That's all. We were only kids.'

'Well, for kids, Mr Cohen, Helen seems to think a little more than necking took place.'

'What does she seem to think?'

'She seems to think you all crawled into the sack.'

'Yeah?'

'Yeah. In fact, she seems to think you all crawled into the sack *together* at one point.'

'Yeah?'

'Yeah. In fact, Mr Cohen, she described what happened as "a regular orgy".'

'Yeah?'

'Yeah. Funny you should forget an event of such proportions, don't you think, Mr Cohen? Unless, of course, you're in the habit of attending org –'

'All right,' Cohen said.

'Is that what happened?'

'Yeah, yeah, that's what happened.'

'You remember it now?'

'Remember it?' Cohen said. 'I've been trying to forget it for twenty-three years. I've been in analysis for six years, trying to forget what happened that night.'

'Why?'

'Because it was disgusting. We were drunk. It was disgusting. It warped my entire life.'

'How?'

'What do you mean, how? Because we turned a – a private thing into a – a circus. That's how. Look, do we have to talk about this?'

'Yes, we have to talk about it. Was everyone drunk?'

'Yeah. Randy Norden was a kind of wild kid. He was older than most of us, you know, in his twenties, already in law school. His parents had this big penthouse apartment on Grover, and they were away in Europe, so we all went up there after the show. The girls got pretty high. I guess Helen was setting the pace. Well, you've seen her, you know the kind of girl she is. She was the same then.'

'Hold it right there, Mr Cohen!' Meyer said sharply.

'What? What's the matter?'

'How do *you* know what kind of girl she is, Mr Cohen? When did *you* see her last?'

'I haven't seen anybody connected with that show since I got out of college.'

'Then how do you know what she looks like now?'

'I don't.'

'Then why'd you say she's the same now as she was then?'

'I just assumed she'd be. She was a wild one then, and the wild ones don't change.'

'How about the other girls?'

'They – were just nice kids. They got drunk, that's all.'

'And what happened?'

'Well, we ... it was Randy's idea, I guess. He was older, you know, and with Helen, and naturally ... well, we all split up ... there were a lot of bedrooms in the house ... and well ... that's what happened.'

'*What* happened?' Meyer insisted.

'I don't want to talk about it!' Cohen shouted.

'Why?'

'Because I'm ashamed of it, that's why. Okay?'

'Tell us about being a sniper, Mr Cohen,' Carella said.

'That was a long time ago.'

'So was the party. Tell us about it.'

'What do you want to know?'

'What theatre of operations?'

'The Pacific.'

'Where?'

'Guam.'

'What'd you use?'

'A BAR with a telescopic sight.'

'Smokeless powder?'

'Yes.'

'How many men did you kill?'

'Forty-seven,' Cohen said without hesitation.

'How'd you feel about it?'

'I hated every minute of it.'

'Then why didn't you get out?'

'I asked for a transfer, but they said no. I was a good sniper.'

'These were Japanese you killed?'

'Yeah, Japanese.'

'How much did you drink at that party?'

'A lot.'

'How much?'

'I don't remember. We *really* began drinking after Richardson left. There was a lot of booze. Tony was in charge of tickets ...'

'Tony?'

'Forrest. Tony Forrest. He was in charge of tickets for the show, and I think he took some money from the till to pay for the party. It wasn't illegal or anything, I mean everybody in the group knew he was doing it. It was for the party. But there was a lot of booze.' Cohen paused. 'Also, there was a climate of ... well, the war had already started in Europe, and I guess most students at the time knew America would get into it sooner or later. So it was a kind of kiss-me-my-sweet attitude. We didn't care what the hell happened.'

'Did you shoot from a tree or what?' Kling asked suddenly.

'What?'

'When you were on Guam.'

'Oh. Usually. Yeah.'

'What happened afterwards?' Carella asked.

'It depended on the operation. Usually, I was supposed to pin down ...'

'After Helen and Randy started the ball rolling, I mean.'

'We all got involved.'

'And after that?'

'We wound up in one room.'

'Which room?'

'Randy's mother's room. The bedroom. The big one.'

'Where were you on Friday, May fourth?' Meyer asked.

'I don't know.'

'Try to remember.'

'When was that?'

'It was Friday, May fourth. This is Wednesday, May ninth. Where were you, Cohen?'

'I think I was out of town.'

'Where?'

'Upstate. That's right. I left Friday morning. Just to take a long weekend, you know?'

'You wouldn't have been in Minneapolis on May fourth, would you?'

'Minneapolis? No. Why should I go there? I've never been there in my life.'

'Do you remember a man named Peter Kelby?'

'Yeah, he was in the play.'

'Did he come to the party?'

'He came to the party.'

'Where'd you stay last weekend? On your trip upstate?'

'I went fishing.'

'We didn't ask you what you did, we asked you where you stayed.'

'I camped out.'

'Where?'

'In the reservation. Up near Cattawan.'

'In a tent?'

'Yes.'

'Alone?'

'Yes.'

'Anyone else on the camp site?'

'No.'

'Stop for gas anywhere along the way?'

'Yes.'

'Use a credit card?'

'No.'

'You paid cash?'

'Yes.'

'The same in any restaurants you might have stopped at?'

'Yes.'

'In other words, Mr Cohen, we have only your word that you were up in Cattawan and not in Minneapolis, Minnesota, killing a man named Peter Kelby.'

'Whaaat!'

'Yes, Mr Cohen.'

'Look, I . . .'

'Yes, Mr Cohen?'

'Look . . . why would I . . . how the hell would I even know where Peter Kelby *was*? I mean . . .'

'Somebody knew where he was, Mr Cohen, because somebody put a bullet in his head. We rather suspect it was the same somebody who killed six people right here in this city.'

'I haven't seen Peter Kelby since we were in school together!' Cohen protested. 'I had no idea he was in Minneapolis.'

'Ah, but, Mr Cohen, *somebody* found out he was there. In fact, Mr Cohen, it couldn't have been too difficult because even a nice lady named Agnes Moriarty at Ramsey University was able to find out where Kelby lived – and she wasn't even interested in murdering him.'

'Neither was I!' Cohen shouted.

'But that party still bugs you, huh, Cohen?'

'Why does it bug you?'

'Too much sex there?'

'You enjoy firing a rifle?'

'How does it feel to kill a man?'

'Which girl were you with, Cohen?'

'What else did you do that night?'

'SHUT UP, SHUT UP, SHUT UP!' Cohen shouted.

The squad-room was very silent. Into the silence, Carella said, 'What's your analyst's name, Cohen?'

'Why?'

'We want to ask him some questions.'

'Go to hell,' Cohen said.

'Maybe you don't realize how tight your position is, Cohen.'

'I realize, all right. But whatever is said between me and my analyst is *my* business, and not yours. I had nothing to do with any of these goddamn murders. You can go around opening whatever closets you want to, but some of my closets are going to stay *closed*, you hear me? Because they've got nothing to do with you *or* your case, they've only got to do with *me*. You hear that? Me. David Arthur Cohen, a crummy gag-writer who doesn't know how to laugh, all right? I don't know how to laugh, all right, that's why I'm going to an analyst, okay? And maybe I didn't know how to laugh even back in nineteen forty when I was eighteen years old and at a wild party that should have knocked me out, but that doesn't mean I'm going around killing people. I killed enough people. I killed forty-seven people in my life, and they were all Japanese, and I cry every night for every goddamn one of them.'

The detectives stared at him for several moments, and then Meyer nodded his head at the other men, and they walked to one corner of the room and stood shoulder to shoulder in a tight huddle.

'What do you think?' Meyer asked.

'I think this is real meat,' Carella said.

'Yeah, it looks that way to me, too.'

'I'm not sure,' Kling said.

'Shall we book him?'

'We've got nothing that'll stick,' Carella said.

'We don't have to book him for homicide. Let's throw something else at him, just to keep him here a while. I think he'll crack if we can keep at him.'

'What can we book him for? Vagrancy? He's gainfully employed.'

'Dis cond.'

'What did he do?'

'He used abusive language just a little while ago.'

'What do you mean?'

'He told you to go to hell.'

'Jesus, that's slim,' Carella said.

'We just gonna let him walk out of here?'

'How long can we hold him without booking him?'

'If the thing comes to trial, it's up to the court to decide what was a proper and reasonable length of time. But, man, if this comes up zero, he'll sue for false arrest before we can bat an eyelash.'

'If we don't book him, we're not arresting him, are we?' Kling asked.

'Sure we are. If we keep him from leaving here, that amounts to arrest. He'd have a bona-fide case against the city, and against the arresting officer.'

'So what the hell do we do?'

'I think we ought to ring in the D.A.'s office,' Carella said.

'You think so?'

'Absolutely. Call the Homicide Bureau, tell them we've got what looks like real meat, and we want a D.A. in on the questioning. Let them make the decision.'

'I think that's best,' Meyer said. 'Bert?'

'Let's work him for another ten minutes, see what we can get on our own.'

'I don't think so.'

'Okay, do what you like.'

'Steve, you want to call the bureau?'

'Yeah, sure. What do we do with him meanwhile?'

'I'll take him downstairs.'

'Not in the cells, Meyer!'

'No, no, I'll phony it up, stall him. I don't think he knows anything about booking, anyway.'

'All right,' Carella said.

Meyer walked across the room. 'Come on, Cohen.'

'Where are you taking me?'

'Downstairs. I want you to look at some pictures.'

'What kind of pictures?'

'Of the people killed by the sniper.'

'Why?'

'I think you ought to see them. We want to make sure they're the same people who were in that play.'

'All right,' Cohen said. He seemed immensely relieved. 'Then can I go?'

'You better look at the pictures first.'

He started out of the squad-room with Meyer and Kling, passing another man in the corridor outside. The man was perhaps forty-five years old, small and round with sad brown eyes and a rumpled brown suit. He walked to the railing and stood just outside it, holding his hat in his hands, waiting to be discovered.

Carella, who had already dialled the bureau and was at the desk nearest the railing, glanced up at the man, and then turned his attention back to the telephone conversation.

'No, we haven't booked him,' Carella said. 'We've got nothing that'll stick yet.' He paused, listening. 'No, he hasn't said a thing, denies the whole business. But I think we can get him to crack if we work on him. Right. Can you get a man down right away? Well, how long can we legally hold him here? That's just my point. I think the decision should come from someone in the D.A.'s office. Well, when's the soonest? That's too late. Can't you get someone here this morning? Okay, fine, we'll be waiting.'

He hung up and turned to the man.

'Yes, sir, can I help you?'

'My name is Lewis Redfield,' the man said.

'Yes, Mr Redfield?'

'I hate to bother you this way ...'

'Yes?'

'... but I think my wife may be in danger.'

'Come in, Mr Redfield,' Carella said.

Redfield nodded, took a hesitant step towards the railing, searched it for an opening, and then stopped dead in his tracks, bewildered. Carella went to the gate and opened it for him.

'Thank you,' Redfield said, and then waited for Carella to lead him to the desk.

When they were seated, Carella asked, 'What makes you think your wife is in danger, Mr Redfield? Has she received any threatening ...?'

'No, but I ... this may sound silly to you.'

'What is it, Mr Redfield?'

'I think this fellow may be after her.'

'What fellow?'

'The sniper.'

Carella wet his lips and stared at the small round man opposite him. 'What makes you think that, Mr Redfield?'

'I've been reading the papers,' Redfield said. 'The people who've been killed ... they were all in a play with Margaret many years ago.'

'Margaret *Buff*? Is that your wife's maiden name?'

'Yes, sir.'

'Well!' Carella smiled and extended his hand. 'It's certainly good to see you, Mr Redfield. We've been trying to locate your wife.'

'I would have come sooner, but I wasn't sure.'

'Where *is* your wife, sir? We'd like very much to talk to her.'

'Why?'

'Because we have what looks like a good suspect, and any information ...'

'You've found the killer?'

'We're not sure, Mr Redfield, but we think we have.'

Redfield sighed heavily. 'I'm certainly relieved to hear that. You have no idea the strain I've been through. I was certain that at any moment Margaret would ...' He shook his head. 'I certainly am relieved.'

'*Could* we talk to her, sir?'

'Yes, of course.' Redfield paused. 'Who did you arrest? Who's the man?'

'His name is David Arthur Cohen,' Carella said. 'But he hasn't been arrested as yet, sir.'

'Was he in the play, too?'

'Yes.'

'Why was he doing it? Why was he killing all those people?'

'We're not sure yet. We think it had something to do with a party he went to.'

'A party?' Redfield asked.

'Well, it's pretty complicated, sir. That's why I'd like to talk to your wife.'

'Of course,' Redfield said. 'The number is Grover 6–2100. I think you can reach her there now.'

'Is that your home number, sir?'

'Yes, it is.'

'Will she be able to come down here right away?'

'I think so, yes.'

'You have no children, sir?'

'What?'

'Children. Will she have to make arrangements? If so, I can go ...'

'No. No children.' Quickly, Redfield added, 'We've only been married a short time.'

'I see,' Carella said. He pulled the phone to him and began dialling.

'Two years, actually. I'm Margaret's second husband.'

'I see.'

'Yes, she divorced her first husband in nineteen fifty-six.'

Carella put the receiver to his ear and listened to the ringing on the other end. 'We're anxious to get her down here because we've either got to book Cohen for homicide or let him go. A man from the D.A.'s office is coming up soon, and anything concrete we can provide him with will be a big help. Your wife just might be able to ...'

'Hello?' a woman's voice said.

'Hello, Mrs Redfield?'

'Yes?'

'This is Detective Carella of the Eighty-seventh Squad. Your husband is here with me, Mrs Redfield. We've been trying to locate you on these sniper killings.'

'Oh. Oh, yes,' she said. Her voice was curiously toneless.

'I wonder if you could come down to the station house. We have a suspect, and we're very anxious to talk to you.'

'All right.'

'Can you come down right now?'

'All right.'

'Fine, Mrs Redfield. When you get here, just tell the desk sergeant you want to see me, Detective Carella, and he'll pass you through.'

'All right. Where is it?'

'On Grover Avenue, right opposite the park's carousel entrance.'

'All right. Is Lewis there?'

'Yes. Do you want to speak to him?'

'No, that's all right.'

'We'll see you soon then.'

'All right,' Margaret Redfield said, and then she hung up.

'She's coming over,' Carella said.

'Good,' Redfield answered.

Carella smiled and put the phone back into its cradle. It rang almost instantly. He pulled the receiver up again and said, 'Eighty-seventh Squad, Carella.'

'Carella, this is Freddie Holt, the eight-eight across the park.'

'Hi, Freddie,' Carella said cheerfully. 'What can I do for you?'

'You still working on the sniper case?'

'Yeah.'

'Good. We got your boy.'

'What?' Carella said.

'Your boy, the guy who's been doing it.'

'What do you mean?'

'We picked him up maybe ten minutes ago. Shields and Durante made the collar. Got him on a rooftop on Rexworth. Shot two ladies in the street before we could pin him down.' Holt paused. 'Carella? You with me?'

'I'm with you,' Carella said wearily.

Chapter Sixteen

The man in the cage in the squad-room of the 88th Precinct was a raving lunatic. He was wearing dungarees and a tattered white shirt, and his hair was long and matted, and his eyes were wild. He climbed the sides of the small mesh prison like a monkey, peering out at the detectives in the room, snarling and spitting, rolling his eyes.

When Carella came into the room, the man in the cage shouted, 'Here's another one! Shoot the sinner!'

'That the man?' Carella asked Holt.

'That's him, all right. Hey, Danny!' Holt called, and a detective sitting at one of the desks arose and walked to where Carella and Holt were standing.

'Steve Carella, Danny Shields.'

'Hi,' Shields said. 'I think we met once, didn't we? That fire over on Fourteenth?'

'I think so, yeah,' Carella said.

'Don't go too near the cage,' Shields warned. 'He spits.'

'Want to fill me in on it, Danny?' Carella said.

Shields shrugged. 'There's not much to tell. The beat cop called in about a half-hour ago – it was about a half-hour, huh, Freddie?'

'Yeah, about that,' Holt said.

'Told us some nut was up on the roof shooting down into the street. So Durante and me, we took the squeal, and he was still blasting away when we got there. I went up the hallway, and Durante took the building next door, to go up the roof, you know, catch him by surprise. By the time we got up there, he'd plugged two dames in the street. One was an old lady, the other was a pregnant woman. They're both in the hospital now.' Shields shook his head. 'I just spoke to the doctor on the phone. He thinks the pregnant one's gonna die. The old

156

lady has a chance, he says. That's the way it always is, huh?'

'What happened on the roof, Danny?'

'Well, Durante opened fire from the next building, and I come in and got him from behind. He was some bundle, believe me. Look at him. He thinks he's Tarzan.'

'Shoot the sinners!' the man in the cage yelled. 'Shoot all the filthy sinners!'

'Did you get his weapon?'

'Yeah. It's over there on the desk, tagged and ready to go.'

Carella glanced at the desk. 'That looks like a twenty-two,' he said.

'That's what it is.'

'You can't fire a three-oh-eight slug from that,' Carella said.

'Who said you could?'

'Well, what makes you think this is my boy?'

'We figured it was a chance. We been getting a lot of heat on this, Carella. The loot got a call from downtown only yesterday, asking if we was really helping you guys or just fooling around up here.'

'I don't think he's connected with it,' Carella said.

'Well, what do you want us to do?'

'Have you checked his apartment yet?'

'What apartment? He probably sleeps in the park.'

'Where'd he get a rifle?'

'We're checking our stolen guns list now. There was a couple of hockshops busted into, night before last. Maybe he done it.'

'Have you questioned him yet?'

'Questioned him? He's got a screw loose, all he does is yell about sinners and spit at anybody who goes near him. Look at him, the crazy bastard.' Shields looked at him, and then burst out laughing, 'Jesus,' he said, 'just like a monkey, look at him.'

'Well, if you find out where he lives, run a check for me, will you? We're looking for any gun that might have fired a three-oh-eight Remington.'

'That's a lot of guns, buddy,' Shields said.

'Yeah, but it's not a twenty-two.'

'That's for sure.'

'You'd better call Buenavista and tell them to warm up a bed in the psycho ward.'

'I already done it,' Shields said. 'Not your boy, huh?'

'I don't think so.'

'Too bad. I'll tell you the truth, Carella, we were a little anxious to get rid of him.'

'Why? Nice sweet old guy like that.'

'Well, we got a problem, you see.'

'What's the problem?'

'Who's gonna take him out of that cage?' Shields asked.

*

Margaret Buff Redfield was waiting for Carella when he got back to the squad-room.

She was thirty-nine years old, and she looked tired. Her hair was brown, and her eyes were brown, and she wore a shade of lipstick too red for her complexion, and a dress that hung limply from her figure.

She took Carella's hand wearily when her husband introduced them, and then looked at him expectantly, as if waiting for him to crack her across the face. Suddenly, Carella had the notion that this woman had been hit before, and often. He glanced at the soft-spoken Redfield, and then turned his attention back to Margaret.

'Mrs Redfield,' he said, 'there are some questions we'd like to ask you.'

'All right,' Margaret said.

Intuitively, Carella turned to Redfield and said, 'Sir, if you don't mind, I'd like to talk to your wife privately.'

'Why?' Redfield said. 'We're married. We have no secrets.'

'I know that, sir, and I respect it, believe me. But we've found that people will often be very nervous in the presence of their husbands or wives, and we try to conduct an interview privately, if it's at all possible.'

'I see,' Redfield said.

'Yes, sir.'

'Well ...'

'If you don't mind, sir, I'll ask Miscolo to show you to a room down the hall. There are some magazines in there, and you can smoke if you ...'

'I don't smoke,' Redfield said.

'Or perhaps Miscolo can bring you a cup of coffee.'

'Thank you, I don't want a . . .'

'Miscolo!' Carella yelled, and Miscolo came running at the double. 'Would you show Mr Redfield down the hall, please, and make him comfortable?'

'Right this way, sir,' Miscolo said.

Reluctantly, Redfield got out of his chair and followed Miscolo out of the squad-room. Carella waited until he was certain Redfield was out of earshot, and then he turned to Margaret and quickly said, 'Tell me about the party in nineteen forty.'

'What?' she said, startled.

'The party at Randy Norden's house.'

'How . . . how did you know about that?' she asked.

'We know about it.'

'Does my husband know?' she asked quickly.

'We didn't ask him, Mrs Redfield.'

'You won't tell him, will you?'

'Of course not. We only want to know about David Arthur Cohen, Mrs Redfield. Can you tell me how he behaved that night?'

'I don't know,' she said. She moved back on the seat of the chair, and her voice came from her throat like a whine, as though he were holding a club and were threatening her with it. Her eyes had widened, and she visibly moved deeper into the chair, her back climbing it, her shoulders pulling away from him.

'What did he do, Mrs Redfield?'

'I don't know,' she said, and again the words were a whine, and her eyes were beginning to blink uncertainly now.

'Mrs Redfield, I'm not asking you what *you* did that night. I only want to know . . .'

'I didn't do anything!' she shouted, and she gripped the sides of the chair with both hands, as though knowing he would hit her now, and bracing herself for the shock.

'No one said you did, Mrs Redfield. I only want to know if anything happened that might have caused Cohen to . . .'

'Nothing happened,' she said. 'I want to go home now. I want my husband.'

'Mrs Redfield, we think we have a murderer downstairs. He

claims he had nothing to do with the murders, but if we can find something, anything, that'll start him talking . . .'

'I don't know anything. I want to go home.'

'Mrs Redfield, I don't want to have to . . .'

'I don't know anything.'

'. . . embarrass you, or make this difficult for you. But unless we can find something concrete to . . .'

'I told you, I don't know. I want to go home. I don't know.'

'Mrs Redfield,' Carella said evenly, 'we know everything that happened that night at Randy Norden's. *Everything*. Helen Struthers told us about it, and so did Cohen.'

'I didn't do anything. They did it.'

'Who?'

'The . . . the others.'

'What others?'

'Helen and Blanche. Not me. Not me.'

'What did they do?'

'They couldn't get me to do it,' Margaret said. 'I wouldn't, and they couldn't force me. I knew what was right. I was only seventeen, but I certainly knew what was right and what was wrong. It was the others, you see.'

'You had no part of anything that happened, is that right?'

'That's right.'

'Then why didn't you leave, Mrs Redfield?'

'Because they . . . they held me. All of them. Even the girls. They held me while . . . listen, I didn't even want to be in the *play*. I was Mag, the barmaid, she was a barmaid, not a girl like the others, my mother wouldn't let me be in the play at first because of the kind of girls they were supposed to be, I was only in the play because Randy talked me into it. But I didn't know the kind of boy Randy was until the night of the party, when he was with Helen. That's what started it all, his being with Helen, and everybody drinking so much . . .'

'Were you drunk, Mrs Redfield?'

'No, yes, I don't know. I must have been drunk. If I'd been sober, I wouldn't have let them . . .'

Margaret stopped.

'Yes?'

'Nothing.'

'Mrs Redfield, do you want to tell this to a policewoman?'

'I have nothing to tell.'

'I'll get a policewoman.'

'I have nothing to say to her. What happened wasn't my fault. I've never ... do you think I *wanted* what happened?'

'Miscolo, get me a policewoman, on the double!' Carella yelled.

'The others did, but not me. I was drunk, or they wouldn't have been able to hold me. I was only seventeen. I didn't know about such things because I came from a good home. If I hadn't been drunk ... I wouldn't have let them ruin my life. If I'd known the kind of boy Randy was, the kind of filth in him, in his body, and the others, Helen especially, if I'd known what she was, I wouldn't have stayed at the party, I wouldn't have had a single drink, I wouldn't even have been in the play, if I'd known what kind of boys they were, and girls, if I'd known what they could do to me, if I'd only known. But I was seventeen, I didn't even think about such things, and when they said they were going to have a party after the show, I thought it would be a nice party, after all Professor Richardson was going to be there, but they were drinking even with him in the room, and then when he left, it must have been about midnight, they really began drinking, I'd never even drunk anything stronger than beer before that, and here they were pouring drinks, and before I knew it, only the six of us were left ...'

Alf Miscolo saw the policewoman going down the corridor towards the squad-room, and he figured it wouldn't be long before he could stop the pretence of entertaining Lewis Redfield. Redfield had tired quickly of even the new *Saturday Evening Post*, and he fidgeted uneasily in his chair now in the sparsely furnished, loosely titled 'reception room' which was really a small cubicle off the Clerical Office. Miscolo wished both Redfield and his wife would go home so that he could get back to typing and filing, but instead the policewoman vanished down the corridor, and Redfield sat in his chair and fidgeted as though his wife were in the hands of heartless torturers.

Miscolo was a married man himself, so he said, 'Don't worry about her, Mr Redfield. They're only asking a few questions.'

'She's a nervous woman,' Redfield answered. 'I'm afraid they might upset her.' He did not look at Miscolo as he spoke. His eyes and his complete attention were riveted to the open doorway leading to the corridor. He could not see the squad-room from where he sat, nor could he hear a word spoken there, but his eyes stayed on the hallway, and he seemed to be straining to catch stray snatches of sound.

'How long you been married, sir?' Miscolo asked, making conversation.

'Two years,' Redfield said.

'You're practically newlyweds, huh?' Miscolo said, grinning. 'That's why you're so worried about her. Me, I been married . . .'

'I don't think we fall into the "newlywed" category,' Redfield said. 'We're not exactly teenagers.'

'No, I didn't mean . . .'

'Besides, this is my wife's second marriage.'

'Oh,' Miscolo said, and couldn't think of anything to add to it.

'Yes,' Redfield said.

'Well, plenty of people get married late in life,' Miscolo said lamely. 'Lots of times, those turn out to be the best marriages. Both parties are ready to accept family responsibility, ready to settle . . .'

'We don't have a family,' Redfield said.

'I beg your pardon?'

'We don't have any children.'

'Well, sooner or later,' Miscolo said, smiling. 'Unless, of course, you don't want any.'

'I'd like a family,' Redfield said.

'Nothing like it,' Miscolo answered, warming to his subject. 'I've got two kids myself, a girl and a boy. My daughter's studying to be a secretary at one of the commercial high schools here in the city. My son's up at M.I.T. That's in Boston, you know. You ever been to Boston?'

'No.'

'I was there when I was in the navy, oh, this was 'way back even before the Second World War. Were you in the service?'

'Yes.'

'What branch?'

'The army.'

'Don't they have a base up near Boston someplace?'

'I don't know.'

'Seems to me I saw a lot of soldiers when I was there.' Miscolo shrugged. 'Where were you stationed?'

'How much longer will they be with her?' Redfield asked suddenly.

'Oh, coupla minutes, that's all. Where were you stationed, Mr Redfield?'

'In Texas.'

'Doing what?'

'The usual. I was with an infantry company.'

'Ever get overseas?'

'Yes.'

'Where?'

'I was in the Normandy invasion.'

'No kidding?'

Redfield nodded. 'D-day plus one.'

'That musta been a picnic, huh?'

'I survived,' Redfield said.

'Thank God, huh? Lotsa guys didn't.'

'I know.'

'I'll tell you the truth, I'm a little sorry I missed out on it. I mean it. When I was in the navy, nobody even dreamed there was gonna be a war. And then, when it *did* come, I was too old. I'd have been proud to fight for my country.'

'Why?' Redfield asked.

'*Why?*' For a moment, Miscolo was stunned. Then he said, 'Well ... for ... for the future.'

'To make the world safe for democracy?' Redfield asked.

'Yeah. That, and ...'

'And to preserve freedom for future generations?' There was a curiously sardonic note in Redfield's voice. Miscolo stared at him.

'I think it's important my kids live in freedom,' Miscolo said at last.

'I think so, too,' Redfield answered. 'Your kids and my kids.'

'That's right. When you have them.'

'Yes, when I have them.'

The room went silent.

Redfield lighted a cigarette and shook out the match. 'What's taking them so long?' he asked.

∗

The policewoman who spoke privately to Margaret Redfield was twenty-four years old. Her name was Alice Bannion, and she sat across the desk from Mrs Redfield in the empty squad-room and listened to every word she said, her eyes saucer-wide, her heart pounding in her chest. It took Margaret only fifteen minutes to give the details of that party in 1940, and during that time Alice Bannion alternately blushed, turned pale, was shocked, curiously excited, repulsed, interested, and sympathetic. At one o'clock, Margaret and Lewis Redfield left the squad-room, and Detective 3rd/Grade Alice Bannion sat down to type her report. She tried to do so unemotionally, with a minimum of involvement. But her spelling become more and more uncontrolled as she typed her way deeper into the report and the past. When she pulled the report out of the typewriter, she was sweating. She wished she hadn't worn a girdle that day. She carried the typewritten pages into the lieutenant's office, where Carella was waiting. She stood by the desk while Carella read what she had written.

'That's it, huh?' he asked.

'That's it,' she said. 'Do me a favour next time, will you?'

'What's that?'

'Ask your own questions,' Alice Bannion said, and she left the office.

'Let me see it,' Lieutenant Byrnes said, and Carella handed him the report:

DETECTIVE DIVISION SUPPLEMENTARY REPORT	SQUAD	PRECINCT	PRECINCT REPORT NUMBER	DETECTIVE DIVISION REPORT NUMBER	PAGE NUMBER
	87	87	87-934	RL-4105	1

DETAILS

Mrs. Redfield highly distrubed, did not wish to discuss matter at all. Claimed she had only told this to one other person in her life, her family doctor, and that because of urgency of matter, and need to do something about it. Has retained doctor over the years, general practicioner, Dr. Andrew Fidio, 106 Ainsley Avenue, Isola.

Mrs. Redfield claims drinks were forced upon her against will night of party Randolph Norden's home, circa April, 1940. Claims she was intoxicated when other students left at one or two in morning. Knew party was getting wild, but was too dizzy to leave. She refused to take part in what she knew was happening in other rooms, staying in living room near piano. Other two girls, Blanche Lettiger and Helen Struthers, forced Mrs. Refield into bedroom, held her with assistance of boys while Randy Norden "abused" her. She tried to get out of room, but they tied her hands and one by one attacked her until she lost consciousness. She says all the boys participated in attack, and she can remember girls laughing. She seems to recall something about a fire, one of drapes burning, but memry is hazy. Someone took her home at about five a.m., she does not remember who. She did not report incident to sole living parent, mother, out of fear.

In circa October 1940, she went to Dr. Fidio with what seemed routine irritation of cervix. Blood test showed she was venereally infects, and that gonorrhea had entered chronic stage with internal scarring of female organs. She told Dr. Fidio about party in April, he suggested prosecution. She refused, not wanting mother·to know about incident. But severity of symptoms indicated hysterectomy to Fidio, and she was admitted hospital in November, when he performed operation. Mother was told operation was an appendectomy.

Mrs. Redfield feels to this day Rany Norden was boy who "diseased" her, but does not know

for sure because each boy was attacker in turn.
She stronly implies unnatural relations with
girls as well, but will not bring self to discuss
it. She said she was glad the boys were dead.
When told that Blanche Lettiger had later become a prostitute, she said, "I'm not surprised." She ended interview by saying, "I
wish Helen was dead, too. She started it all."

DATE OF THIS REPORT

May 9th

Det/3rd   Bannion   Alice R.   7045   87th Squad

RANK   SURNAME   INITIALS   SHIELD NUMBER   COMMAND

SIGNATURE OF COMMANDING OFFICER

They worked on David Arthur Cohen for four hours, putting
him through a sort of crash therapy his analyst would never have
dreamed of. They had him tell and retell the details of that party
long ago, read him sections of the report on Margaret Redfield,
reread it, asked him to tell what had happened in his own words,
asked him to explain the drapes being on fire, asked him what the
girls had done, went over it and over it until, weeping, he could
bear it no longer and simply repeated again and again, 'I'm not
a murderer, I'm not a murderer.'

The assistant district attorney who had been sent up from downtown had a small conference with the detectives when they were
finished with Cohen.

'I don't think we can hold him,' the assistant D.A. said. 'We've
got nothing that'll stick.'

Carella and Meyer nodded.

'We'll put a tail on him,' Carella said. 'Thanks for coming up.'

They released David Arthur Cohen at four o'clock that afternoon. The detective assigned to his surveillance was Bert Kling.
He never got to do any work because Cohen was shot dead as he
came down the precinct steps into the afternoon sunshine.

Chapter Seventeen

There were no buildings across the street from the station house; there was only a park. And there were no trees behind the low stone wall that bordered the sidewalk. They found a discharged shell behind the wall, and they assumed that the killer had fired from there, at a much closer range than usual, blowing away half of Cohen's head. Kling had immediately run out of the muster room, and down the precinct steps, and across the street into the park, chasing aimlessly along paths and into bushes, but the killer was gone. There was only the sound of the whirling carousel in the distance.

The precinct patrolmen were beginning to think this was all very funny. A guy getting killed on the steps of the station house was a pretty macabre piece of humour, but they enjoyed the fun of it nonetheless. They were all aware that the detectives upstairs had called in the D.A. that afternoon, and they were also aware that Cohen had been held in the squad-room for a damn long time, and they joked now about the fact that he could no longer bring charges of false arrest since someone had very conveniently murdered him. One of the patrolmen jokingly said that all the detectives had to do was wait long enough and then everybody who'd been in that play would be dead, and the killings would automatically stop, and they could all go home to sleep. Another of the patrolmen had a better idea. He figured it was simply a process of elimination. As soon as the killer had murdered everybody but *one*, why then the remaining person was obviously the murderer of all the others.

Carella didn't think it was so funny. He knew that neither Thomas Di Pasquale nor Helen Vale had put that bullet in Cohen's head because they both were being escorted around the city by patrolmen who never let them out of sight. On the other hand, Lewis and Margaret Redfield had left the squad-room at one o'clock, some three hours before Cohen walked down those steps and into a Remington .308 slug. Detective Meyer Meyer was sent promptly to the Redfield apartment on the corner of Grover and Forty-first in Isola, where he was told that Margaret Redfield had gone directly to the beauty parlour after leaving the squad-room, apparently feeling in need of treatment after her cathartic experience. Lewis Redfield told Meyer he had gone to his office on Curwin Street after leaving the squad-room, and stayed there until 5 p.m. at which time he had come home. He could remember, in fact, dictating some letters to his secretary, and then attending a meeting at 3 p.m. A call to the office verified the fact that Redfield had come to work at about one-thirty and had not left until five. They could not say where he was specifically at four o'clock when Cohen was murdered, but there seemed little doubt he was somewhere in the office. Nonetheless, because that narrow margin of doubt did exist, Meyer phoned Carella at the squad-room to tell him he was going to stick to the Redfields for a while. Carella agreed that the tail was a good idea, and then he went home to dinner. Neither he nor Meyer thought the case was very funny. In fact, they were sick to death of it.

And then, oddly, considering how lightly the patrolmen were taking all this grisly slaughter, it was a patrolman who provided the next possibility for action in the case, and then only indirectly through a call from Captain Frick at eleven o'clock that night, while Carella was home and trying to read the newspaper.

When he heard the phone ring, he glanced at it sourly, rose from his easy chair in the living-room and quickly walked into the foyer. He picked the receiver from the cradle and said, 'Hello?'

'Steve, this is Captain Frick. I didn't wake you, did I?'

'No, no. What is it?'

'I hate to bother you on this, but I'm still here at the office, and I'm trying to get these time-sheets straightened out.'

'What time-sheets are those, Marshall?'

'On my patrolmen.'

'Oh, yes. Well, what is it?'

'Well, I've got Antonino listed as being with this Helen Vale woman from eight this morning until four this afternoon when he was relieved by Boardman, who'll be on until midnight. That right?'

'I guess so,' Carella said.

'Okay. And Samalman was supposed to be with this guy Di Pasquale from eight this morning until four this afternoon, but I see here on his time-sheet he left at three. And I see that Canavan, who was supposed to relieve him at four, called in at nine p.m. to say he had just relieved on post. Now I don't get that, Steve. Did you give these guys permission for this?'

'What do you mean, Marshall? Are you saying nobody was with Di Pasquale from three o'clock this afternoon to nine o'clock tonight?'

'That's what it looks like. Judging from these time-sheets.'

'I see,' Carella said.

'Did you give them permission?'

'No,' Carella said. 'I didn't give them permission.'

❋

Thomas Di Pasquale had a patrolman at his door and a woman in his apartment when Carella arrived that night. The patrolman moved aside to allow his superior to ring the doorbell. Carella rang it with dispatch, and then waited for Di Pasquale to answer the ring. Di Pasquale's dispatch did not equal Carella's since he was all the way in the bedroom at the other end of the apartment, and he had to put on a robe and slippers and then come trotting through six rooms to the front door. When he opened the door, he looked out at a face he had never seen before.

'Okay, what's the gag?' he asked.

'Mr Di Pasquale?'

'Yeah?'

'I'm Detective Carella.'

'That's very nice. Do you know it's eleven-thirty at night?'

'I'm sorry about that, Mr Di Pasquale, but I wanted to ask you some questions.'

'Can't they wait till morning?'

'I'm afraid not, sir.'

'I don't have to let you in, you know. I can tell you to go whistle.'

'You can do that, sir, that's true. In which case I'd be forced to swear out a warrant for your arrest.'

'Hey, sonny boy, you think you're dealing with a hick?' Di Pasquale said. 'You can't arrest me for anything, because I haven't *done* anything.'

'How about suspicion of murder?'

'How about it? There's no such crime as *suspicion* of anything. Murder? Don't make me laugh. Who am I supposed to have killed?'

'Mr Di Pasquale, can we discuss it inside?'

'Why? You afraid of waking the neighbours? You already woke *me* up, what difference will a few dozen others make? Argh, come in, come in. No damn manners, the police in this lousy town. Come around the middle of the night. Come in, for Chrissake, don't stand there in the hall.'

They went into the apartment. Di Pasquale turned on a light in the living-room, and they sat facing each other.

'So?' he said. 'You're here, you got me out of bed, so say what's on your mind.'

'Mr Di Pasquale, a man was shot and killed this afternoon at four o'clock as he was leaving the police station.'

'So?'

'Mr Di Pasquale, we checked with the patrolman who was assigned to "protect" you, and he tells us you let him go at three o'clock this afternoon. Is that right?'

'That's right.'

'Is it also true that you told him you wouldn't be needing him again until nine o'clock this evening? Is that also true, Mr Di Pasquale?'

'That's true. So what? Is that why you come knocking on my door in the middle of the night? To check on whether or not your patrolman is telling the truth? Is that all you've got to do with your time? You're the guy who called me up at seven-thirty one morning, ain't you? You *like* waking people up, don't you?'

'Mr Di Pasquale, why'd you tell the patrolman you wouldn't need him?'

'For the very simple reason that I was up at Columbia Pictures today talking a deal with the head of the story department. I went up there at three o'clock, and I expected to be there with him until six, at which time I knew we would both go downstairs where a chauffeured Cadillac would be waiting to take us to a very fancy restaurant where I wouldn't be sitting near any windows. We would have a couple of drinks at the bar, and at seven o'clock we would be joined by a writer who would give a story line to the head of the story department, and then we would eat dinner, also not sitting near any windows. Then we would get right into the Cadillac again, and they would drive me home where I asked that fathead patrolman to meet me – I see he isn't even here, there's some other jerk outside – and where also the young lady who is now asleep in the other room would be waiting for me. So you see, Mr Carella who likes to wake up people in the middle of the night, I thought I would save the city a little money and also release a cop for active duty in spots all over the city where teenagers are bashing each other's heads in, instead of hanging around me when I knew I'd be absolutely safe, *that's* why, Mr Carella. Does that answer your question?'

'Were you anywhere near the precinct today, Mr Di Pasquale?'

'I was up at Columbia all afternoon, and then I went straight to dinner, and then I came straight here.'

'Mr Di Pasquale, do you own any guns?'

'No.' Di Pasquale stood up angrily. 'What is all this, would you mind telling me? How come I'm suddenly a suspect in this thing? What's the matter? You running out of people?'

He had delivered his words in anger, but he had struck very close to the truth. They *were* running out of people. They had begun the case by grasping at straws, and they were still grasping at straws.

Carella sighed heavily. 'I suppose the head of Columbia's story department can corroborate . . .'

'You want to call him from here? I'll give you his home number. Go ahead, why don't you call him? You might as well wake up the whole gaddamn city while you're at it.'

'I think that can wait until morning,' Carella said. 'I'm sorry I disturbed you. Good night, Mr Di Pasquale.'

'Can you find your way out?' Di Pasquale asked sarcastically.

*

It was close to the witching hour.

Meyer Meyer stood on the corner opposite the Redfields'

apartment building, and wondered if he should call it a day. He had positioned himself on the street corner at six that evening, and it was now eleven-forty, and he was certain the Redfields would turn out their lights soon and go to sleep. But at seven that evening, Margaret Redfield had come down into the street with a Welsh terrier on a leash, and she had walked around the block and then returned to the building at seven twenty-five. Meyer did not own a dog, but he was sure a seven-o'clock constitutional would not be the final promenade for a terrier kept in a city apartment. And yet, it was now eleven-forty – he glanced at his watch, no, eleven forty-five – and there was no indication that either Margaret or Lewis Redfield would take the pooch down for another stroll before retiring, and besides it was beginning to rain.

It was not a heavy rain at first; it was only a light, sharp drizzle that penetrated directly to the marrow. Standing on the corner, Meyer looked up again at the lighted third-floor apartment window. He swore mildly under his breath, decided to go home, changed his mind, and crossed the street to stand under the awning outside a bakery. The bakery was closed. It was nearing midnight, and the streets were deserted. A strong wind suddenly came in off the river, pushing heavier rain clouds ahead of it. The deluge covered the street. The drizzle turned to a teeming downpour in a matter of seconds. Lightning streaked the sky over the tops of the buildings. Meyer stood under the awning and thought of a warm bed with Sarah beside him. He cursed the Redfields again, decided to go home, remembered that damn Welsh terrier, convinced himself the dog would be going for another walk, pulled up the collar of his coat, and again looked up at the lighted third-floor window. The awning leaked. He glanced up at the tear in the canvas, and then switched his scrutiny back to the window.

The light went out.

There was what seemed like a half-hour of blackness, and then another light went on, the bedroom, he figured, and then a light came up behind a smaller window. The bathroom, Meyer thought. Thank God, they're finally going to sleep. He waited. Both lights stayed on. On impulse, he walked across the street rapidly and into the building. The elevator was directly opposite the entrance doorway. He walked half-way into the lobby and looked up at the indicator over the closed elevator doors. The needle was stopped at the number six. He watched patiently for several moments, and suddenly the needle began to move. Five, four, three ... the needle stopped again.

Three, he thought. The Redfields live on the third floor.

The needle was moving again.

He raced out of the building and crossed the street, taking up his position under the leaking awning, certain now that either Lewis or Margaret Redfield was coming downstairs with the dog before going to bed, and then wondering what the hell difference it made, and then wishing again *he* were home in bed. He kept his eyes on the doorway to the building. Margaret Redfield came out of the doorway, leading the terrier on a leash, just as the patrolman rounded the corner.

It was five minutes to midnight.

The patrolman glanced at Meyer as he passed him, took in the hatless, bald-headed man with the jacket collar turned up, standing outside a closed bakery, five to midnight, rain, empty streets...

The patrolman turned back.

*

The sniper was out of breath.

He had leaped the airshaft between the two buildings, and taken up his position behind the parapet, looking down into the street now, the street empty and deserted, but knowing that she would soon turn the corner, knowing she would soon stroll leisurely up the block, leading the dog, knowing she would soon be dead, breathing hard, waiting.

The rifle felt long and lethal in his hands, more lethal because of the telescopic sight, bringing the street below into sharp focus. He sighted along the barrel at the lamp-post in the middle of the block, far below, close to him because of the sight, she would make a good target.

He wondered if he should stop.

He wondered if she should be the last one, and then wondered if she shouldn't have been the first one. He knew the dog would lead her to the lamp-post. He knew she would stop there. He fixed the lamp-post in the crossed hairs of the sight, and cursed

173

the rain. He had not supposed the rain would make that much difference, and yet he could not see too clearly, he wondered if he should wait until another time.

No.

You bastards, he thought.

You, he thought.

I should have taken care of you first.

The rain drummed on his shoulders and his head. He was wearing a black raincoat, wearing the night around him, hidden by the night, he felt a thrill of anticipation as he waited for her. Where are you, he thought, come walk into my rifle, come walk into my sight, come let me kill you, come, come, come.

*

The dog stopped alongside the fire hydrant on the corner. He sniffed, hesitated, sniffed again. Meyer, who was watching Margaret and the dog intently, didn't even see the patrolman approaching.

'What's the trouble, mister?' the patrolman said.

'Huh?' Meyer answered, startled.

'What are you standing around here for?'

A grin came onto Meyer's face. Of all times for a cop to get conscientious, he thought, and then he said, 'Look, I'm . . .'

The patrolman shoved him. The patrolman had just come on duty, he had a little heartburn, and he wasn't ready to take any crap from a suspicious character who looked as if he was planning a burglary. 'Move along,' he said angrily. 'Go on, move along.'

'Look,' Meyer said, the grin dropping from his face. 'I happen to be a . . .'

'You gonna give me trouble?' the patrolman asked, and he grabbed Meyer's right sleeve, twisting it in his fist.

At that moment, Margaret Redfield disappeared around the corner.

*

He saw her turn into the block. She was partially obscured by the rain, but he recognized her and the dog immediately.

He wiped the palms of his hands on his coat, realizing only afterwards that the coat was wetter than his hands.

I'm going to kill you better than the others, he thought.

You bitch, I am going to kill you better.

He was no longer out of breath, but his heart was pounding furiously, and his hands had begun to tremble. He glanced over the parapet again, saw that she was coming steadily down the block.

There was a lot of wind. He would have to compensate for the wind.

He wiped the rain from his eyes.

He put the rifle to his shoulder.

He sighted again on the lamp-post, waiting.

Come on, he thought.

Come on.

Goddamn you to hell, *come on*!

∗

'I'm a detective,' Meyer said. 'Let go of my sleeve!'

Instead of letting go of Meyer's sleeve, the patrolman twisted his arm up behind his back and began frisking him for a gun, which of course he found immediately.

'You got a permit for this?' he asked, while across the street Meyer could see nothing, could hear only the clatter of Margaret's heels around the corner.

'You goddamn fool,' Meyer said to the patrolman. 'You want to find yourself walking a beat in Bethtown? Give me that gun!'

The patrolman suddenly recognized something in Meyer's voice, a note of authority, a no-nonsense attitude that told him he might indeed be walking a beat in Bethtown if he didn't co-operate with this bald bastard. He handed back the .38 immediately. Lamely, he said, 'You can understand . . .' But Meyer wasn't in an understanding mood, nor did he even hear the patrolman's words. He ran to the corner and turned it immediately. He could see Margaret Redfield half-way up the street, the dog hesitating near the lamp-post, close to the kerb. He began walking after her, ducking into doorways. He was perhaps a hundred feet from her when she suddenly collapsed on the sidewalk.

He had heard no shot.

She fell swiftly and soundlessly, and the absence of sound magnified the event because he knew she had been shot, and yet there was no clue to the sniper's hiding-place. He began running towards her, and then stopped, and then looked up at the roof-tops on either side of the street, and realized suddenly that the shot could have come from any one of them. The terrier was barking now, no, not barking but wailing, a lonely terrible wail like the mournful sound of a coyote.

The woman, Meyer thought. Get to the woman.

The roof, he thought, get to the roof.

Which roof?

Where?

He stopped dead in the middle of the street.

The killer is up there somewhere, he thought, and his mind stopped working for a moment. The rain drumming around him, Margaret Redfield lying on the sidewalk ahead of him, the dog wailing, the patrolman coming around the corner curiously, Meyer's mind clicked shut, he did not know what to do or where to turn.

He ran to the doorway of the building closest to the lamp-post, ran reflexively, passing Margaret Redfield who poured blood into the gutter while the dog wailed, ran without stopping to think it through, going there automatically because that was where the shot had most likely come from. Then he stopped on the sidewalk and shut his eyes for a moment, forced reason into his mind, forced himself to realize the killer would not come down on this block, he would leap the airshaft, cross over to one of the other buildings and try to make his escape either on the avenue or the next cross-street.

He ran for the corner. He almost slipped on the slick, wet asphalt, regained his balance, ran with the gun in his right fist, pumping the air with both arms, reaching the corner and turning it, and running past the fire hydrant, and stopping before the entrance to the Redfield's apartment building, and looking up at the still-lighted windows, and then turning his eyes back to the street, and seeing nothing.

Where? he thought. Where are you?

He waited in the rain.

The patrolman discovered the body of Margaret Redfield

around the corner. The terrier snapped at him when he tried to pick up her wrist to feel for a pulse-beat. He kicked the dog in the chops with the side of his shoe, and then lifted her wrist. Blood was pouring down her arm from the wound in her shoulder. She was one hell of a mess, and it was raining, and the patrolman had heartburn.

But he had sense enough to know she wasn't dead, and he immediately phoned the nearest hospital for an ambulance.

The sniper did not come down into the street where Meyer was waiting for him. Nor did Meyer suppose he was still on one of the roofs up there. No, he had guessed wrong, and that was that. The sniper had made his escape elsewhere, swallowed by the rain and the darkness, free to kill again.

As he holstered his gun, Meyer wondered how many mistakes a cop is allowed. Then, dejectedly, he looked up as he heard the sound of the approaching ambulance.

Chapter Eighteen

The hospital was shrouded in a slow, steady drizzle that echoed the greyness of its walls. They arrived there at 1 a.m., parked the car, and then went to the admissions desk where a nurse told them Mrs Redfield was in Room 407.

'Has Mr Redfield arrived yet?' Meyer asked.

'Yes, he's upstairs,' the nurse said. 'Mrs Redfield's doctor is with her, too. You'll have to check with him before talking to the patient.'

'We'll do that,' Carella said.

They walked to the elevator. Carella pressed the call button, and then said, 'Redfield got here fast enough.'

'He was in the shower when I went up to the apartment to tell him his wife had been wounded,' Meyer said. 'Takes a shower every night before going to bed. That explains the bathroom light going on.'

'What'd he say when you told him?'

'He came to the door in a bathrobe, dripping water all over the floor. He said, "I should have taken the dog down myself."'

'That's all?'

'That's all. Then he asked where his wife was, and said he'd dress and get right over here.'

They took the elevator up to the fourth floor, and waited in the corridor outside Margaret's room. In ten minutes' time, a white-haired man in his sixties came out of Room 407. He looked at his watch and was hurrying towards the elevators when Carella stopped him.

'Sir?' he said.

The man turned. 'Yes?'

'Sir, are you Mrs Redfield's doctor?'

'I am,' the man said. 'Dr Fidio.'

'I'm Detective Carella of the Eighty-seventh Squad. This is my partner, Detective Meyer.'

'How do you do?' Fidio said, and he shook hands with the men.

'We'd like to ask Mrs Redfield some questions,' Carella said. 'Do you think she's up to it?'

'Well,' Fidio said sceptically, 'I just gave her a sedative. I imagine it'll begin working any minute. If this won't take too long ...'

'We'll try to keep it short,' Carella promised.

'Please,' Fidio answered. He paused. 'I can appreciate the gravity of what has happened, believe me, but I wish you'd try not to overtax Margaret. She'll live, but she'll need every ounce of strength she can summon.'

'We understand, sir.'

'And Lewis as well. I know you've got to ask questions, but he's been through a great deal in the past month, and now this thing with ...'

'The past month?' Carella said.

'Yes.'

'Oh, worrying about Margaret, you mean.'

'Yes.'

'Well, we can understand the strain he's been under,' Carella said. 'Knowing a sniper was at large and wondering when ...'

'Yes, yes, that too, of course.'

Meyer looked at Fidio curiously. He turned to Carella, and saw that Carella was also staring at the doctor. The corridor outside Room 407 was suddenly very silent.

'That *too*?' Carella said.

'What do you mean?' Meyer said instantly.

'What *else* was bothering him?' Carella asked.

'Well, the entire business with Margaret.'

'*What* entire business, Dr Fidio?'

'I hardly think this is germane to your case, gentlemen. Margaret Redfield was shot and almost killed tonight. This other thing is a private matter between her and her husband.' He looked at his watch again. 'If you're going to question her, you'd better hurry. That sedative ...'

'Dr Fidio, I think *we* ought to decide what's germane to the case, don't you? What was troubling Lewis Redfield?'

Dr Fidio sighed deeply. He looked into the detectives' faces, sighed again, and then said. 'Well . . .' and told them what they wanted to know.

*

Margaret Redfield was asleep when they entered the room. Her husband was sitting in a chair beside her, a round-faced man with sad brown eyes and a dazed expression on his face. A black raincoat was draped over a chair on the other side of the room.

'Hello, Mr Redfield,' Carella said.

'Hello, Detective Carella,' Redfield answered. Behind his chair, rain stained the window, crawling over the glass, dissolving the pane in globs of running light.

'Dr Fidio tells us your wife is going to pull through.'

'Yes, I hope so,' Redfield said.

'It's no fun getting shot,' Meyer said. 'In the movies, it all looks so clean and simple. But it isn't any fun.'

'I don't imagine it is,' Redfield said.

'I take it you've never been shot,' Carella said.

'No.'

'Were you in the service?'

'Yes.'

'What branch, Mr Redfield?'

'The army.'

'Did you see combat?'

'Yes.'

'Then you know how to use a rifle?'

'Oh, yes,' Redfield said.

'Our guess is you know how to use it pretty well, Mr Redfield.'
Redfield looked suddenly alert. 'What do you mean?' he asked.

'Our guess is you were an expert shot during the war, is that right, Mr Redfield?'

'I was only fair.'

'Then you must have learned an awful lot since.'

'What do you mean?' Redfield asked again.

'Mr Redfield,' Meyer said, 'where did you go tonight when your wife left the apartment with the dog?'

'I went into the shower.'

'Which shower?'

'What ... what do you mean ... the *shower*,' Redfield said. 'The shower.'

'In your bathroom ... or on the roof?'

'What?'

'It's raining, Mr Redfield. Is that why you missed killing her? Is that why you only hit her in the shoulder?'

'I don't know what you ... who are you ... my *wife*, do you mean? Are you talking about *Margaret*?'

'Yes, Mr Redfield. We are talking about your knowing your wife would take the dog down sometime before midnight. We are talking about your going up to the roof the moment she left the apartment, and crossing over to a building around the corner, and waiting for her to come around the block. That is what we are talking about, Mr Redfield.'

'I ... that's the silliest thing I've ever heard in my life. Why, I ... I was in the shower when it ... when it all happened. I even came to the door in my bathrobe. I ...'

'How long does it take to shoot someone, get back down to the apartment, and hop into the tub, Mr Redfield?'

'No,' Redfield said. He shook his head. 'No.'

'Yes, Mr Redfield.'

'No.'

'Mr Redfield,' Carella said, 'we just had a chat with Dr Fidio in the hall outside. He told us that you and Mrs Redfield have been trying to have a baby since you were married two years ago. Is that right?'

'Yes, that's right.'

'He also told us that you came to see him at the beginning of April because you thought perhaps something was wrong with you, that you were the one who was responsible.'

'Yes,' Redfield said.

'Instead, Dr Fidio told you that your wife, Margaret, had had a hysterectomy performed in November of nineteen forty, and that she could never have a child. Is that also true, Mr Redfield?'

'Yes, he told me that.'

'And you didn't know about it before?'

'No, I didn't.'

'Surely your wife must have a scar. Didn't you ever ask her about it?'

'Yes. She said it was an appendectomy scar.'

'But when Dr Fidio told you the real nature of the operation, he also told you about a party that had taken place in April of nineteen forty, and about your wife's subsequent venereal ...'

'Yes, yes, he told me,' Redfield said impatiently. 'I don't see what ...'

'How old are you, Mr Redfield?'

'I'm forty-seven.'

'Have you ever had any children?'

'No.'

'You must have wanted them pretty badly.'

'I ... I wanted children.'

'But they made it impossible, didn't they?'

'I ... I ... don't know who you mean, what you mean.'

'The people who were at that party, Mr Redfield. The ones who caused the hysterectomy, the ones ...'

'I don't know who those people were. I don't know what you mean.'

'That's right, Mr Redfield. You *didn't* know who they were. You only knew there had been a party following a production of *The Long Voyage Home*, and you properly assumed all the members of the cast had been to that party. What did you do? Find Margaret's old theatre programme and just start going down the list?'

Redfield shook his head.

'Where's the rifle, Mr Redfield?' Carella said.

'Who was next on your list?' Meyer said.

'I didn't do any of this,' Redfield said. 'I didn't kill any of them.'

'If that's your raincoat,' Carella said, 'you'd better put it on.'

'Why? Where are you taking me?'

'Downtown.'

'What for? I'm telling you I didn't ...'

'We're booking you for homicide, Mr Redfield,' Carella said.

'Homicide? I didn't kill anyone, how can you ...?'

'We think you did.'

'You thought Cohen did, too.'

'There's one difference, Mr Redfield.'

'What's that?'

'This time we're sure.'

*

It was 2 a.m. by the time they got back to the precinct. He tried to brazen it through at first, but he did not know a patrolman was going through his apartment while the detectives were questioning him in the squad-room. He refused to admit a thing. He kept repeating that he was in the shower when his wife was shot, he hadn't known a thing about it until Meyer knocked on his door to report the shooting, and then he'd put on a robe and come to answer it. How could he have been on the roof? And when Cohen was killed on the precinct steps, he had been at work in his office, how could they hold him responsible for *that* death? True, no one had seen him after the time the office meeting broke up at three-thirty, true, he could have left the office by the back stairs and come over to the precinct to wait for Cohen, but wasn't that the wildest sort of speculation, by those rules *anyone* could be convicted of murder, he had nothing to do with any of this.

'Where were you on Friday, May fourth?' Carella asked.

'I was home,' Redfield answered.

'You didn't go to work?'

'No, I had a cold.' He paused. 'Ask my wife. She'll tell you. I was home all day.'

'We *will* ask her, believe me, Mr Redfield,' Carella said. 'As soon as she's able to talk to us.'

'She'll tell you.'

'She'll tell us you weren't in Minneapolis, huh?'

'I've never been there in my life. I had nothing to do with any of this. You're making a terrible mistake.'

And that was when the patrolman walked into the squad-room. Maybe Redfield would have told it all, anyway. It is a convention that they tell it all in the end, and besides human beings will reach a point where hope is balanced against despair, where they see the scale slowly tilting against them. They recognize this point when it arrives, they stare at it with wise discovering eyes, and they know there is nothing left for them. There is relief in confession. If there is any hope at all in despair, it is the hope of confession, so perhaps he would have told it all, anyway.

The patrolman walked directly to Carella's desk. He put down the long leather case and said, 'We found this at the back of his bedroom closet.'

Carella opened the case.

The rifle was a bolt-action Winchester Model 70.

'This your gun, Mr Redfield?' Carella asked.

Redfield stared at the rifle and said nothing.

'These were on the shelf, behind his hats,' the patrolman said. He put the box of Remington .308 cartridges on the desk-top. Carella looked at the cartridges, and then looked at Redfield, and then said, 'Ballistics'll give us the answer in ten minutes' time, Mr Redfield. You want to save us the trouble?'

Redfield sighed.

'Well?'

Redfield sighed again.

'Call Ballistics, Meyer,' Carella said. 'Tell them a patrolman's on his way down with a rifle. We want a comparison test made with the bullets and discharged shells we've got on . . .'

'Never mind,' Redfield said.

'You want to tell us about it?' Carella said.

Redfield nodded.

'Stenographer!' Carella yelled.

'I didn't plan to kill any of them,' Redfield said. 'Not at first.'

'Just a second,' Meyer said. 'Miscolo, you got a stenographer coming?'

'You see,' Redfield said, 'when Dr Fidio told me about Margaret, I . . . I was shocked, of course, I thought . . . I don't know what I thought . . .'

'Miscolo! Goddamnit!'

'Coming, coming!' Miscolo shouted, and he ran into the squad-room and began taking the confession himself, his open pad poised on his lap.

'Sadness, I suppose,' Redfield said. 'I wanted a family, you see. I'm not a young man. I wanted a family before it was too late.' He shrugged. 'Then . . . as I . . . as I began thinking about it, I guess I . . . I began to get . . . angry. My wife couldn't have a baby, you see. She could never have a baby. Because of the

184

hysterectomy. And they were responsible, you see. The ones who had done this to her. The ones who had been at that party Dr Fidio described to me. Only, I ... I didn't know who they were.'

'Go on, Mr Redfield.'

'I came upon the theatre programme by accident. I was looking for something in one of the closets, and I found the trunk, covered with dust, all covered with dust, and the programme was inside it. So you see I ... I knew their names then. I knew the people who had done it to her, the ones who were at the party, and I ... I began looking for them, not intending to kill them at first, but only wanting to see them, wanting to get a good look at the people who had ... who had made it impossible for me to have children, my wife to have children. Then, I don't know when, I think it was the day I found Blanche Lettiger, traced her to that dingy neighbourhood, followed her, and she ... she stopped me on the street and propositioned me, I think it was that day, seeing the filth she had become, and knowing the filth that had poisoned Margaret, I think it was that day I decided to kill them all.'

Redfield paused. Miscolo looked up from his pad.

'I killed Anthony Forrest first, not for any special reason, only because he was the one I decided to kill first, and maybe in the back of my mind I thought it would be better not to kill them in the order they appeared on the programme, but just at random, you know, so it wouldn't seem they were connected, just to kill them, you know, as if ... as if there were no connexion.'

'When did you decide to kill your own wife, Mr Redfield?' Meyer asked.

'I don't know when. Not at the beginning. After all, she'd been a victim of the others, hadn't she? But then, I ... I began to realize how dangerous my position was. Suppose a connexion was made between the murder victims? Suppose you discovered all ten of them had been members of the same college drama group? Why, if I killed them all but allowed Margaret to live, well ... well, wouldn't you wonder about this? Wouldn't you want to know why she alone hadn't been killed? Of the entire group? My position was very dangerous, you see.'

'So you decided to kill her, too? To protect yourself?'

'Yes. No. More than that. Not only that.' Redfield's eyes

suddenly flared. 'How did I know she'd really been such an innocent? Was she really a victim that night? Or had she gone along with the others willingly in their ... their dirty ... I didn't know, you see. So I ... I decided to kill her, too, along with the other ten. That was why I came here to talk with you. To throw off suspicion. I figured if I'd already been to the police to warn them of possible danger to Margaret, why then when she was actually killed, I wouldn't be a suspect, don't you see? That was what I figured.'

'*Were* you in Minneapolis on May fourth, Mr Redfield?'

'Yes. Oh yes, I killed Peter Kelby.'

'Tell us about Cohen.'

'What do you want to know?'

'How you managed the timing on it.'

'That was risky. I shouldn't have attempted it. But it worked, so maybe ...'

'*How*, Mr Redfield?'

'I left here at about one yesterday, and was back in my office by one-thirty. I dictated some letters to my secretary, and then attended a meeting at two forty-five. I said it started at three, but it really started at two forty-five and was over by three-fifteen. I left the office through the back stairs. My own private office has a back door opening on a corridor, you see, and I took the steps down ...'

'No one saw you?'

'No.'

'Did you tell anyone you were leaving?'

'No. I thought of telling my secretary not to disturb me for the next hour or so, but then I decided against it. I thought if anyone started asking questions later, it would be better if everyone simply said they knew I was in the building somewhere, but not exactly where.'

'You did quite a bit of planning, didn't you, Mr Redfield?'

'I was murdering,' Redfield said simply.

'You realize you were murdering?'

'Of course I realize it!'

'Go on. What'd you do when you left the office?'

'I took a cab to my apartment. To get the rifle.'

'Is that where you usually stored it?'

'Yes. In the closet. Where your man found it.'

'Your wife never saw it?'

'Once.'

'Didn't she ask you what you were doing with a rifle?'

'She didn't know it was a rifle.'

'What do you mean?'

'It was in the case. I told her it was a fishing-rod.'

'And she *believed* you?'

'I don't think she has ever seen a rifle *or* a fishing-rod. The gun was in its case. She had no way of knowing what was inside the case.'

'Go ahead. You went to pick up the rifle . . .'

'Yes. I took a cab. I was uptown in twenty minutes, and in another ten minutes I was across the street, waiting in the park. Cohen came out at four o'clock, and I shot him.'

'Then what?'

'I ran south across the park, and took a cab on the other side.'

'Did you take the rifle back to the office with you?'

'No. I left it in a pay locker at Central Station.'

'And picked it up again on your way home last night?'

'Yes. Because I planned to kill Margaret last night, you see. The rain. I missed because of the rain.'

'Where'd you get the rifle, Mr Redfield?'

'I bought it.'

'When?'

'The day I decided to kill them all.'

'And the silencer?'

'I made it from a piece of copper tubing. I was afraid it might injure the barrel of the rifle after a single firing, but it didn't. I think I was lucky. Aren't silencers supposed to ruin guns?'

'Mr Redfield, you killed eight people, do you know that?' Carella said.

'Yes, I know that.'

'Why didn't you adopt children, Mr Redfield? You could have done that, you know. You planned all these murders, but you couldn't see your way clear to going to an adoption agency! Why the hell . . .?'

'It never occurred to me,' Redfield said.

After the confession was typed and signed, after they led Redfield downstairs to the detention cells to await transportation downtown later in the morning, Carella picked up the phone and called Thomas Di Pasquale to tell him he could stop worrying.

'Thanks,' Di Pasquale said. 'What the hell time is it?'

'Five a.m.,' Carella said.

'Don't you *ever* sleep?' Di Pasquale said, and hung up.

Carella smiled and replaced the phone in its cradle. He did not call Helen Vale until later in the day. When he told her the good news, she said, 'Oh, that's wonderful. Now I can go away without that on my mind.'

'Away, Mrs Vale?'

'For summer stock. The season starts next month, you know.'

'That's right,' Carella said. 'How could I forget a thing like that?'

'I want to thank you again,' Helen said.

'For what, Mrs Vale?'

'For the patrolman,' she answered. 'I really enjoyed having him.'

Cynthia Forrest came up to the squad-room that afternoon to pick up the material she had left, the old newspaper clippings, the report cards, the theatre programme. Bert Kling met her in the corridor as she was leaving.

'Miss Forrest,' he said, 'I want to apologize for the way ...'

'Drop dead,' Cynthia said, and went down the iron-runged steps to the street.

The three detectives were alone in the squad-room. May was dying, the long summer lay ahead. Outside on the street, they could hear the sound of a city rushing by, ten million people.

'I keep thinking about what you told me,' Meyer said suddenly.

'What was that, Meyer?'

'When we were leaving Etterman's office, the German guy, the one whose son was shot down over Schweinfurt.'

'Yeah, what about it?'

'You said, "You can't hate a people here and now for what another people in another time did."'

'Mmm,' Carella said.
'Redfield hated them here and now,' Meyer answered.
The telephone rang.
'Here we go,' Kling said, and picked up the receiver.

Ed McBain
Another Part of the City £3.50

Sadie the bag-lady was preparing for a cold night in her favourite
doorway when two masked men drew up outside the Luna Mare
and shot the proprietor.

Homicides were rare in the Fifth Precinct. Just before Christmas they
were unheard of. Detective Reardon, up to his eyes in marital
problems, cursed his luck.

But Reardon was a good cop, and an inquisitive one. He wanted to
know why. Why an unknown Arab was shot at La Guardia. Why a
lawyer lay dead in his apartment. And why a senator was edgy.

Was there a connection with the Luna Mare homicide? And how
many more would die? It looked like it was going to be a long hard
winter for the boys of the Fifth . . .

'Splendidly readable . . . The faces have changed but the structure is
essentially the same: a hyper active plot, a large well-controlled cast
and a tricky puzzle' GUARDIAN

'The random jigsaw comes together with all the gnarled McBain
cunning' OBSERVER